F

"Bursting with imagination! In *Just Emilia*, Jennifer Oko manages to transform a stuck elevator into a black box, a hall of mirrors, and a Swiss Army knife with her astonishing storytelling powers. Three women trapped inside share a past in this entertaining novel about guilt, blame, and the possibility that forgiveness can alter the future."

—Mary Kay Zuravleff, author of *American Ending* and *Man Alive!*

"Jennifer Oko's *Just Emilia* is a deeply moving story, uniquely told, about the different versions of ourselves—past, present, and future—that co-exist, and how, with the correction of long-buried distorted memories, they can finally find peace. A novel I won't soon forget."

—Laura Zigman, bestselling author of *Separation Anxiety* and *Small World*

"Gripping from the start, this novel combines compelling storytelling with mordant humor. I loved it."

—Clare McHugh, author of *The Romanov Brides* and *The Most English Princess*

"*Just Emilia* is a feat of imagination. Oko asks universal questions—how do we make sense of our past and what do we want for our future?—in delightful and inventive ways. Prepare to be surprised and moved as the elevator doors close on Emilia, Millie, and Em. They may be trapped, but the reader is taken on an unforgettable journey through memory, grief, guilt, and hope."

—Miriam Gershow, author of *Closer* and *Survival Tips: Stories*

"What happens when three versions of the same person collide in a dimensional mishap stuns the imagination. Disbelief, anger, humor, fear, redemption, and forgiveness unwind at a pace that keeps readers turning pages. I love this book and can't stop thinking about what it would be like to meet myself at different ages. Readers will ponder the same long after they finish this enchanting story."

—Chris McClain Johnson, author of the Fugere Prize winning novella *Three Guesses*

"*Just Emilia* uniquely stitches together three generations of the protagonist, Emilia, into a novel wholly unlike any other. Steeped in nostalgia and longing, the book invites readers to consider, if given a chance, what you would say to your younger self, and who do you ultimately hope to become? A beautifully written, thought-provoking novel that will remain at the top of my favorites list."

—Kerri Schlottman, author of *Tell Me One Thing*

JUST EMILIA

Jennifer Oko

Regal House Publishing

Published by
Regal House Publishing, LLC
Raleigh, NC 27605
All rights reserved

ISBN -13 (paperback): 9781646035779
ISBN -13 (epub): 9781646035786
Library of Congress Control Number: 2024944623

Cover images and design by © C. B. Royal

Printed in the United States of America

Regal House Publishing, LLC
https://regalhousepublishing.com

For Tula Karras

PART I

1

STEP INSIDE: EMILIA

October 12
11:17 a.m.
Friendship Heights Metro
Washington, DC

I was the last one of us to step in, calling out for the others to *hold the doors, please* as I lunged over the threshold with my myriad shopping bags. I didn't want to wait for the next ride. I was late enough as it was.

"Thanks," I said to no one and everyone, and, without fully registering who was there, I turned around to face the front and wait for the doors to close, which they seemed reluctant to do.

"Could someone push M?" someone asked after a few moments of static silence, the voice tinged with impatience. The old woman I quickly realized it belonged to did not wait for a response. Instead, she reached past me with a knobby finger outstretched like ET's and pushed the round metal button, and then, when that didn't work, she jammed her finger into the "door close" button, the one with the two arrows pointing inward, pressing it until they finally did just that. That seemingly mundane action was what ultimately brought us to where we find ourselves now, dangling over a darkness, boxed into a steel cage, quiet to the rest of the world, and vice versa.

At the time—the moment of the button pressing—none of this seemed at all out of the ordinary. After all, the DC Metro was in a grave state of disrepair, with the city shutting down line after line because of sparks on the tracks and occasional smoke in the trains. Just three months before, a woman had died from smoke inhalation after an electrical fire at Gallery Place, and it

had been only two weeks since an entire train had to be evacu-
ated from the middle of a tunnel near the Navy Yard because it
had simply stopped running. But like so many things, it just felt
like the demands of transporting oneself around a metropolitan area somehow superseded the dangers. One had to get to
work or to school, after all, so best not to think about the fact
that you might not make it home from your evening commute.
Or your shopping excursion. Or whatever.

So for that brief moment, the fact that the doors were slow
to close didn't particularly faze me. It didn't cross my mind that
the elevator's mechanical reluctance might be a good signal to
simply step back out.

But in retrospect, I am not so sure if maybe those doors did
in fact linger open a moment longer than too long, if maybe
I had indeed felt a slight wobble underfoot when I stepped
across the threshold.

I am guessing that the sullen-looking teenage girl currently
sitting across from me remembers it a little differently, but that
is because she probably wasn't paying much attention at that
critical juncture. Sure, she probably remembers hearing someone shout to *hold the doors, please*, and maybe she remembers
that she dutifully waved her hand up and down the doorsill in
order to do just that, but when I charged in with all those bags,
she had to step back to make space, and in that moment of
stepping back she was probably thinking that the middle-aged
woman with the bags—that would be me—was rather rude. I
would have been thinking that too.

But what I mostly remember is that once the doors closed,
the elevator seemed to drop rather than descend. It happened
so fast I couldn't even scream. I couldn't breathe. It felt like a
free fall, like that Falcon's Fury tower in Busch Gardens that
Sonya had somehow gotten me to ride last summer, except this
time we weren't strapped in. This time, the elevator stopped
with a violent jerk, my stomach dropped, and I grabbed for
the handrail but somehow caught the sleeve of the teenager's
sweatshirt instead, and I took her down with me when I fell.

That, I am sure all of us remember, the older woman who extended her hand to me, pulling me back to my feet, the sullen teenager hunched over across from me.

"Are you okay?" all three of us asked in unison, once steady on our feet, and it would have been almost comic except that it wasn't exactly a moment to laugh. And then, as if synchronized, we each brushed ourselves off and said simultaneously, "I'm fine. I'm fine," in mildly defiant tones, and that blurt of *a cappella* actually was worth a laugh. Just a quick one. Because shortly after that the fluorescent light began to flicker.

And then?

Then it was pitch dark.

There was a distant clanking noise, and then it was silent to boot.

"Oh shit," the girl and I both said at once.

The older woman simply gasped, and for a millisecond or a few minutes—it is impossible to know which it was—we each stood motionless, as if frozen in time. What was one to do, after all? It wasn't even possible to see which was the button that would sound the alarm.

"What should we do?" asked the girl, breaking the silence with this logical question.

I dropped all three of my shopping bags so I could rummage around in my oversized suede purse, hating how structureless it was, how things always got lost.

"Got it," I said and tapped my phone so the screen started to glow, and then I swiped up repeatedly in an attempt to turn on the flashlight. "Fuck." I held the device out toward the girl. My hand was shaking so hard I thought I might drop it; she grabbed it and held it up to her face, the blue light briefly illuminating her frightened, darkly rimmed eyes, eyes reminiscent of that Madonna phase I had briefly embraced back in the mid-'80s. I was half certain I would find a stack of simple black rubber bracelets if the girl were to push up the sleeve of her sweatshirt. It's so funny how teen fashion cycles around.

"Can you get the flashlight on?" I asked her, but she didn't respond—silent from shock, I figured—so I snatched it back and dialed 911.

Nothing happened. I tried again. Nothing.

"Do either of you have a phone?" I implored. "I can't get a signal."

Not that I could see them very well, even with the dim blue glow of the screen, but I could make out that they were both shaking their heads, which was flabbergasting in and of itself. Who doesn't have a phone, right? Were the girl's parents so progressive that they'd managed to limit their daughter's digital consumption that far into high school? Or was she grounded for overuse? Some irresponsible post on social media? Was the old woman so old that she didn't have a phone at all? Or was she just too old to know how to use it?

I tried again.

Nothing.

I felt for the elevator's button panel and began to frantically push every one of them, groping around until I felt the braille that I couldn't decipher, and then I felt what could be the outline of a bell. It had to be the alarm. I pressed it hard. Harder.

Nothing.

I stood there in the dark, panic rapidly encroaching.

I counted to slow down my breathing. I focused on the exhale.

Seconds ticked by.

The girl started banging on the door and crying out for help. The old woman and I quickly chimed in, all of us rapidly screaming ourselves hoarse.

Nothing.

"Wait!" the old woman demanded during a break in the noise. "This isn't working. Someone has got to come, right? It's a busy station. They'll have to notice that one of the elevators is broken soon enough."

Maybe.

We stood waiting for another interminable minute before the light suddenly flickered back on, which was a relief, of course, but it was also a bit embarrassing to have my panicked expression suddenly exposed.

"Okay," I said and grabbed the handrail to be ready for the inevitable lurch when the elevator started to move again.

Except that it didn't.

And now?

Now more than thirty minutes have passed.

The Friendship Heights Metro station is located at the top edge of the northwest quadrant of Washington, DC. It's far enough from the city center that if you ascend one of the northern escalators, you get spit out into Maryland. It's a fairly tony spot, with one of the exits leading directly into Neiman Marcus and another exit tunneling under a building that houses a J.Crew, an H&M, and a restaurant run by the brothers who once won that reality show *Top Chef.* Bloomingdale's is just down the street, and one block north, across the Maryland line, is a line of stores including Tiffany's and Jimmy Choo—what passes for DC's Rodeo Drive. Just up from the spate of those fancy stores, medical building after medical building is lined up, offering everything from biopsies to Botox. You might think that most of the folks frequenting these establishments rarely take the Metro, but the parking is limited and the traffic often tricky, so it is in fact a fairly frequented station.

It opened back in 1984, just a couple of years before my mother was killed. It wasn't all that far from our house and my mother had initially fretted about how the development could bring crime into the neighborhood, an unspoken way of suggesting that by creating easy access to our wealthy enclave, some of the other "troubles" of the de facto segregated city might spread. DC may have been the murder capital of the country back then, but it wasn't in our neck of the woods.

My mother grew more excited when she learned that luxury shopping would be part of the deal because, for her, identity was a very external matter. "You should dress for who you want to be, not for who you are," she would regularly tell me, who, more often than not, was dressed in ripped-up jeans tucked into heavy black lace-up boots, topped off with an oversized sweatshirt with a neckline so stretched out it draped asymmetrically over one of my shoulders, like the actress from *Flashdance*, Jennifer Beals. "Emilia, you look like a destitute swamp monster," my mother would say, or something along those lines. "Now, I am sure that's not really your aspiration, is it?"

It wasn't, but then again, I didn't know what was. I did know, however, that I didn't want to be an on-air television reporter like her, partly because for my mother wearing starchy tailored clothing was a job requirement. I still remember the live shot that she had done from the Metro station, which was typical of the inventive little things that had sealed her reputation as a broadcast pioneer. My mother, Sally Fletcher, was the darling anchor of the morning news, back when most show hosts were cemented behind their lacquered desks.

The halo of platinum blond could be seen as she recited what became her catchphrase, "Hello, America! Today is a brand new day!" I watched that segment on the boxy television set that for years teetered precariously on our kitchen counter as my mother emerged into the frame wearing a bright orange-yellow blazer with a matching fitted skirt. On anyone else it would have conjured up images of carrots, but Sally Fletcher could make a potato sack look elegant. She had the long neck of a dancer and legs that could have belonged to someone half her age, and her sapphire-blue eyes always capped off whatever it was that she was wearing like a finishing touch. It was one of those snapshot moments of childhood that never fully made sense. Why did that particular image sear itself into my memory and not something else?

I don't recall why my mother did the live shot from the Metro. For a national news program, a local subway station opening shouldn't have warranted attention, but there she will forever be in my brain, ascending an escalator and appearing on the mezzanine level like some sort of revelation. It is a memory that keeps her as luminous and imperious in death as she was in life.

But memory is fallible. I know that as well as anyone. So maybe it didn't really happen at all.

Regardless, my mother is one of the reasons why I always prefer to take the elevator. It bothers me to remember her that way. Also, there is the fact that half the time the escalators aren't running anyway and at hundreds of feet below the sidewalk, there are a lot of steps to go down.

That said, this morning the entrance to the elevator had seemed curiously foreboding. The vertical bars of the gate that separated the sidewalk from the platform looked as if they had been repurposed from a prison, and a stream of sunlight cast jagged, ominous shadows like something out of *The Cabinet of Dr. Caligari.*

The girl would later make the same analogy. She said she had recently seen that classic silent horror film in her history elective, *The Early Age of Cinema*, and she had been in that kind of mood. She'd had that kind of morning. The ambiance was befitting the darkness she was feeling, she told me; it was a pathetic fallacy—a term she had learned in AP English. That was where I had first learned it too. It is a deeply imprinted, decades-old snapshot of mine—my pretty, young teacher, Ms. Callahan, pacing in front of the green chalkboard while she described how the tumultuous weather reflected the characters in Emily Brontë's *Wuthering Heights.*

The old woman, too, would tell me that she hadn't been in the best of head spaces herself when she arrived on the platform, and the clattering screech of the elevator's chains had intensified the anxiety that had been rising in her chest since earlier that morning when she had decided it was time to go and have it out with her daughter once and for all. That was where she was headed, she would tell us later, to her daughter's apartment near the Woodley Park station, just a few stops away.

I, however, had been rushing too fast to absorb any of this symbolism; at my moment of arrival I was just anxious to get back to my house where I had more than a few things to attend to. All I noticed was that something seemed off when the doors were about to close.

Which is to say, the external realities each of us had been experiencing earlier in the day were very different from what we've been experiencing since we walked into this elevator. We each had our own motivations that had brought us here, things that we were each running to or from, but inside the elevator all of that momentum came to a screeching halt and each of our interior realities slammed up against the cold steel walls.

Newton's First Law of Motion. The girl said she had studied it in physics class. An object in a state of motion will remain in a state of motion unless an external force acts upon it.

And that, in a manner of thinking, is what happened.

The elevator plunged into the dark, and we each lost our way.

2

MORNING EDITION, PART 1: EMILIA

October 12
7:30 a.m.
Upper Northwest
Washington, DC

Earlier this morning, as with every morning, at exactly 7:30 the theme song for NPR's *Morning Edition* came blaring from the old clock radio on my bedside table. I'd had the clock since my twelfth birthday; I held on to it the way some people hold on to a nostalgically tacky decorative plate or a childhood toy. To get it, I had quite literally broken my ceramic piggy bank and gathered up the dust-covered coins to go to the White Flint Mall in a taxi with my best friend Amy—the taxi fare being my mother's great treat as she'd rather have died than be spotted at that low-rent shopping center. The oversized neon-blue digits on the clock face had caught my adolescent eye when we walked past Radio Shack, and I decided that it was that, and not yet another sweater from Benetton—the original target of the shopping spree—that was worth blowing my savings over. That same clock radio has since woken me up almost every day of my life, although the audio output has changed over time. Instead of catchy tunes of '80s-era indie-pop, this morning it was broadcasting about new rape allegations against Harvey Weinstein, wildfires spreading across California, and President Trump carrying on about the evils of the Affordable Care Act.

It was all a bit much to take in before coffee, but the radio was in its third decade of use, covered with scratches and prone to channeling static, which is why on this particular morning after the national news headlines fizzled to a whirring buzz, I did not hear the weather update forecasting rain in the early afternoon, nor did I hear the long list of Metro delays and scheduled repairs.

By the time the static reverted to the local newscast with a reporter describing a neighborhood tree-planting initiative, my pajamas were crumpled in a heap on the bathroom floor and I was stepping into the shower. The news made me think about the yawning hole in front of our house where an old ginkgo tree had once stood, a conspicuous gap in the long row of ginkgo trees that graced the grass strips in front of every other house on the street, a signature touch of the 1929 housing developer. Ours had been taken down years ago, long before any of the current residents lived on the block, but we had never replaced it and the break in the otherwise lush canopy was a source of consternation among this new generation of neighbors.

After yet one more complaint, this one from a young family that had only recently moved in across the street, Joel—my husband—had finally had enough. He hightailed it over to the absurdly overpriced Johnson's Nursery a few blocks down Wisconsin Avenue and returned with foliage bursting out from the back of our Prius. He had the idea to put a maple sapling in the empty space—not a ginkgo tree, he knew better than that—as well as two more maples in the front yard, because why not? In addition to appeasing our pissy neighbors, it was an opportunity, part of his ongoing effort to make this "our" house rather than my family's "ancestral" home, even though we had been living in it together for almost ten years now, ever since my father passed away and I inherited the large brick colonial along with everything else. But Joel and I fought about the layout of the trees, unable to agree if one should go a little over here or a little over there, and so now, four days later, the saplings still lay on their sides with the roots drying out inside their burlap bundles.

Of course, the fight wasn't really about the trees, it was about so much else. It was about Joel's discomfort in living amidst so many of my dead parents' belongings and my irritation that he was so willing to erase them, as if the fact that I liked to display my mother's china made me some kind of morbid fetishist. He hadn't wanted to live in the house in the first place. He wanted to sell it and create a home of our own. Start fresh. But the real estate market being what it was and our combined incomes being what they were, that didn't make sense. And so now, about a decade later, here we were. The house was a time warp and our relationship was frayed. The fight was about that.

Over the next few days we settled into a chilly truce, trying to be nice to each other in front of our eleven-year-old daughter, Sonya, asking about her homework and eating family meals like all happy families, but last night even that had blown up into a misdirected torrent.

"Rose, bud, thorn!" Sonya demanded at dinner as per hump night—Wednesday night—tradition. Each of us had to list one happy thing, one thing we were looking forward to, and one thing we would like to improve. It was something a teacher had implemented in Sonya's Montessori preschool class, and for almost a decade it had been a cherished family tradition. Even as an increasingly petulant pre-teen, Sonya still wanted to play along. But last night, I really didn't.

"Not today, sweetie," I said. "I'm too tired."

"Come on, Emilia," Joel said with a heavy sigh. "It's not a heavy lift."

Maybe not for you, I thought, but out loud, for Sonya's sake, I relented. "Fine," I said, and I could see Sonya relax into her chair. Sonya loved this moment; she had no poker face about that. As an only child, more often than not the good stuff was about her and she couldn't suppress the anticipatory grin when it was my turn to go.

I smiled back. In some ways my daughter was still untarnished by the coming onslaught of adolescence. She never recoiled from a compliment the way I used to when I was that age, on the few occasions that my mother had actually said anything nice.

"Sonya," I said, "you are, as always, my rose. I loved watching you play soccer this weekend. I saw how you comforted your teammates after you lost, and that made me proud." I looked up, consciously making eye contact with her because I'd read in some parenting article somewhere that I should be doing more of that. Sonya's eyes were sapphire blue, depending on the light, which, along with the wavy blond hair, was just one of the many alluring traits that seemed to have skipped a generation. My own eyes are as brown as my hair. Sometimes I wondered how Sonya could even be mine, even though, if pressed, I would have to admit that she was the spitting image of my mother.

"You are a really good sport and a good friend," I continued. "My bud..." For this I had to dig deep. I reached under the table to pet Ruth—our aging Bernedoodle, named in honor of the Supreme Court justice—while I came up with something to say.

"I don't know, I guess I'm looking forward to Halloween." We were planning to do a joint costume year, maybe Wonder Woman and her mother Queen Hippolyta. I embraced this opportunity, even though I knew that once the other girls joined in, I would be relegated to the back of the pack, trying to make small talk with the other cast-off mothers while we nursed bad wine in red plastic cups.

"And thorn?" Sonya asked, egging me on.

"Thorn. That's easy." I shot a look at Joel. "Just look at the front yard."

"Jesus," Joel said.

"It was a joke, Joel."

"Bullshit."

"Joel!" I said, my gaze darting back toward our daughter.

"She's heard worse. Anyway, I'd be more ashamed of your behavior than my language."

"What are you talking about?"

"What am I talking about? How about modeling some respect? Or, I don't know, how about just loosening up for a change?"

"Loosening up?"

"Oh, come on. You'd think I was suggesting planting a forest and not just a couple of trees. 'But my family home!'" he said in a high-pitched falsetto. "'Oh dear, how can I change anything? What would they think? The shade they cast will block my mother's peonies.'"

"Fuck you, Joel," I spat back.

"May I be excused?" Sonya asked and picked up her plate without waiting for an answer. Ruth padded after her into the kitchen, hopeful she might drop some of that half-eaten dinner.

"Nice, Emilia," Joel said when our daughter was out of earshot. "Really nice. Maybe you should just dump out her Zoloft while you're at it."

"What?"

"Isn't that what Dr. Griffith said? That this shit"—he waggled a finger between us—"isn't helping with her anxiety?"

"I'm not the one who's overreacting here. It was a fucking joke. Maybe you're the one who should loosen up."

"Maybe, when our daughter's around you should stop putting our marital thorns on display."

"Okay, fine. You want a different thorn? Tomorrow is the anniversary of my mother's death. Maybe you could cut me some slack."

"Are you kidding?" Joel asked.

"Am I kidding? No, tomorrow is October 12."

"Yes, I know that. But so what?"

"So what? Come on, that's not fair."

"No, *you* come on. Jesus, it's been, what, thirty years?"

"Thirty-one."

"Thirty-one. Even worse. That's a long time, Emilia. People lose parents. I get it. I've gotten it for a long, long time. But I am married to you, not your mother. You can't wave that flag every time you want to duck responsibility for something. It's getting tiresome."

I was dumbfounded. We had been married for almost fifteen years and had known each other even longer than that, and never once had Joel thrown my mother's death in my face. Not like this, anyway. He was usually sympathetic, at least in a quiet way. He never asked about it, never pressed for details surrounding the circumstances of her death, so I'd never had to explain much. Normally, he accepted the mood swings this day usually conjured with patience and delicacy, and for me that was enough.

Joel's reaction at dinner last night was neither patient nor delicate.

Which was why he'd wound up sleeping in the guest room and why, on this morning, the thirty-first anniversary of my mother's death, after I heard the report on the radio about the tree-planting project, after I got dressed and brushed my teeth, I stomped down the stairs and into the kitchen where my husband and daughter were chomping on Cheerios, and announced that I had something to say. It wasn't like a "the truth will set you free" sort of thing that I was going for. It was just that the bickering and tension had come to a head. And something about the conflation of my mother's death with the dying maple trees out front woke me up. It was time to tell them both the whole truth. Sonya was old enough, and Joel, well, our relationship wasn't getting any better, but I couldn't imagine that anything I said at this point could make things any worse.

"Yes?" Joel said as he sipped from the oversized coffee cup that had once belonged to my father. World's Best Dad.

Sonya was munching on cereal but fixated on her iPhone lying on the counter next to her. Text messages were lighting up one after the other.

"Could you put that away, squeak?" I asked.

Sonya flipped the phone over so she couldn't see the screen, but she kept her hand resting on it as if the alerting vibrations were messages unto themselves.

"So," I exhaled. "First. I'm sorry about last night. Sonya, that wasn't fair to you." Sonya shrugged, so I went on. "I've been thinking about it, Joel, and you were right. Just plant the trees wherever you like."

"Thank you, I guess. If they aren't already dead." Joel stood up to get himself more coffee. "Want some?" he said, holding up the carafe like an olive branch.

"No, wait," I said. "That's not it. I mean, there's something else."

Joel glanced at his watch. I took a deep breath.

"So you know what today is, right? October 12th?"

The other two nodded, a little bit bored, a little bit anxious to get on with things. Get back to the phone. Get out the door. Which made perfect sense. They didn't get it. How could they?

"There are some things I've never told you."

"Is your mom actually alive?" Sonya perked up, an impish grin spreading across her face.

"Don't be smart," Joel admonished her.

"It's okay," I said. "But, no, Sonya, she is very much not."

"Okay, so?"

"So, there's more to the story."

Sonya nodded patiently, resigned. I had told her a little about the car crash on our annual drive to the site of the crime. We would head east down New York Avenue and keep going until we could smell the sea air, parking the car near the old vacation house we no longer owned, and then we'd walk three miles of country roads until we reached the Bay Breeze Bridge.

It was a ritual I had started after my father passed away. He never wanted to make a big deal of this day; he just said my mother would have wanted our lives to go on, so after he was gone too, I took the opportunity to begin to try to figure out how to make amends with my mom. Or at least make some sort of amends with how she died. Off I went every year, often taking Sonya along for the ride while she was still young enough to skip school without it being a big deal.

This year we had agreed it didn't make sense anymore,

seeing as it was Sonya's first year of middle school. But there had been a routine. On those walks I would tell Sonya stories about my mother—only the good ones. I would tell her about how people used to stop my mother when we were walking down the street, about how beautiful she was, about how she threw enormous parties and sometimes let me take sips of the fancy wine. I told her about the time my mother let me sit in the anchor seat in the news studio and how, even though she was a terrible cook she did a great job faking it on the show, and how we would laugh about that with Ruby, our nanny and housekeeper, as if all three of us were in on a big joke.

"You've told us a lot already, Emilia," Joel said, with a glance toward the clock. They had to leave in three minutes or Sonya would miss her bus.

"I've never told you the full story."

"Oh," Joel said. "Now this is getting interesting," He placed his mug on the counter and rocked back on his heels.

"Don't mock me, Joel."

"How about finding a better time to talk about whatever this is about when we aren't so rushed?"

"Right. That's part of it. That's what I wanted to ask. Maybe Sonya can just go in late. You too. I was thinking we could talk on the drive. If we left now, we'd be back before lunch."

"I have a test in science," Sonya said quietly.

"What?"

"She said she has a test," Joel said.

"So?" I asked. "Isn't this more important?"

Neither my husband nor my daughter said anything. Time stretched. Then Joel started to laugh.

"Well, if we weren't sure what we were going to talk about at couples counseling this afternoon, we now have plenty of fodder," he said sotto voce. "Come on, Sonya," he said, now sounding all chipper and upbeat. "I'll just drive you to school. Emilia, I'm not sure when I'll be back."

Sonya followed her father out, glancing back only when she got to the end of the hall.

"Sorry, Mom," she said.

The door clicked and I was alone.

I looked at my watch. It would take a couple of hours to drive to the Bay Breeze Bridge. I had to get there, with or without them.

I unplugged my phone from the charging station and wrote Joel a text.

Can you come straight back? I need the car.

He didn't respond. Not to that message. Not to the next.

"Damn it," I said out loud and grabbed the keys to the beater we kept in the garage. The registration had expired, and it hadn't been driven in a year. I backed out of the driveway and was in the middle of the street when the engine died.

After the tow truck came and the dealership called to say they were out of loaners, I gave up. Fine, I figured, maybe this was the universe's way of saying that if I wanted to remember my mother on this day, if I wanted to try to resolve things between us, I needed to do something else. So I decided to engage in some retail therapy at a few overpriced stores. It's what she would have wanted, I reasoned. Because, honestly, it probably would have made more sense to sprinkle my mother's ashes at Neiman Marcus in the first place.

3

INTERNAL PRESSURE: EMILIA

October 12
11:51 a.m.
Friendship Heights Metro
Washington, DC

The light is erratic. It flickers on and off chaotically, sometimes sticking one way or the other for minutes on end, sometimes just for a few seconds. Initially, there are a few perfunctory "are you okays" and "oh shits" between the three of us, but then the light goes out and the darkness sinks us into silence.

It is just so dark.

There isn't even a thin beam forcing its way through the seams of the door. Nothing seeps in from the top. The darkness is so thick I can almost feel it. It's like there is a pressure to it. It's completely disorienting, as if I am deep underwater with no sense of which way is up.

When the light finally does flicker back on, it does so in intermittent flashes so that even the smallest movement resembles a poorly done stop-motion animation.

Then there is a slight buzzing sound and the light once again flickers off, thrusting us back into darkness. The space between the three of us feels increasingly ill-defined as the moments tick forward. We could be three feet apart. We could be ten. It is hard to tell.

I am trying—not all that successfully—not to worry too much about how much time this is taking. The counseling appointment isn't for a couple of hours, but I would very much like to go home first. Clean up. Wash up. Maybe blow out my hair. It wouldn't be the thing that smooths things over between me and Joel, but not showing up to couples counseling looking like a ragged, stressed-out lunatic certainly couldn't hurt.

I try to settle into the silence.

The other two each sneeze and sniffle every now and then, but otherwise there is only the sound of our breathing as each one waits for someone else to say something, offer some wisdom that might help us escape.

When countless minutes later the light finally buzzes back on, the brightness is momentarily blinding.

I blink and look around.

The girl looks familiar to me somehow, but with the hood of her oversized dark-green sweatshirt now shadowing her face, it is hard to know why. Maybe it's just that she is the archetype of a sulky teenage girl, recognizable to anyone. I was so uncomfortable in my skin when I was that age. It pains me to even think about it, because whenever I do, it all feels so disappointing and sad. The girl looks just like that. She sits with her knees tucked against her chest, the hem of her sweatshirt brushing the ground, the tips of her heavy-soled black boots poking out. It almost looks as if she is legless. The mascot of my old high school, the prowling cat baring its teeth, is emblazoned across the front, and I think that there is an odd sort of cosmic humor to be stuck inside an elevator, this elevator in particular, with such a bad memory.

The old woman finally sits down. She uses her black patent leather purse as a cushion, awkwardly splaying her legs out in front of her, her glasses swaying at the bottom of a chain necklace.

I have settled into my own corner, shifting my buttocks onto one of my overstuffed shopping bags, sitting cross-legged, and I wonder if I should try to meditate with the app I downloaded a few weeks back but haven't yet used.

But that would be weird. Plus, God only knows how long we will be stuck in here. I should try to preserve the battery. Instead, I try to calm myself by thinking of other things—of the dry cleaning I meant to pick up; of what I should buy for dinner at the Whole Foods next to my Metro stop when I finally get out. But then I think, no, after this incident, it would be a fine night to order in.

"That looks soft," says the girl. This is the first thing any of us has said in quite some time, and it takes me by surprise.

"What?"

"Your jacket. It looks soft. And warm."

"It is." I have wrapped myself in my new shearling jacket—the equivalent of a full week of the after-school babysitter's pay lost to the Bloomingdale's spring sale and purchased only after much consternation and rationalization—it isn't much more ethical than fur, after all. Now it is simply a cushion against the chill of the metal walls. I glance up from my corner, both grateful for and irritated by the inconsistent light. I am sure I look awful. We all do. The older woman looks miserable, and Lord knows the poor girl looks rather listless, as best as I can make out, what with the hood and the hair hanging over her face.

"Are you cold?" I ask, unable to swat away a swelling maternal sense of concern.

"Bored is more like it," says the girl, nudging her overstuffed backpack with her booted foot. "I can't even listen to music. The battery died."

The older woman chuckles softly. "I am sure this is not the most scintillating experience you've ever had," she says. "But just think. A few years from now, maybe even a few months, it will just be an amusing story for you to tell. You could even write your college essay about this, if you wanted to."

"I already know what I'm going to write about," the girl tartly replies.

"Well, then." The old woman forces a smile. "And you?" she asks me. "How are you holding up?"

"A little worried," I say, although the truth is that I am not worried about myself so much; I am worried about the impression my apparent silence might be having on Joel. If he calls and I don't answer, it will seem that I'm the one being passive-aggressive, that I'm the one who is dodging the confrontation that is just begging to happen, not him. And if the babysitter—but don't call her a babysitter or Sonya will bristle, just call her the helper, I remind myself—if the helper can't reach me or if Sonya wants to talk—at some point soon someone is going to start to get concerned, and in my house, at least with my daughter, concern can spiral fairly rapidly to full-blown anxiety, and as that builds it will be harder and harder for any one of us to remain levelheaded. I can already hear Joel blaming me because our daughter has taken to sobbing under her covers yet again. The headache—or the stomachache or backache, or really just pick an ailment—wouldn't have manifested if I had only answered my phone. It's killing me that I can't just text to say that I'm fine, that I'm sorry about how we all left things this morning, that I can't possibly be stuck in here for all that much longer (not to mention how nice it would be to just call for help).

"What time is it, anyway?" the girl asks.

I tap the screen on my phone, which has been sitting idle on top of the emptied Bloomingdale's bag. It is 12:02 p.m. There's almost no way I am going to make it back in time for our appointment. Joel is going to have a field day with this one.

"It's been almost an hour," I say, and it is the last thing any one of us says for a while.

The girl sighs audibly and shakes her head the way a dog might after a bath. The hood of her sweatshirt slips back, and her long bangs fall in front of her face. I remember hiding behind a fringe just like that when I was around the same age. I noticed, when the light first flickered on, that I actually looked a lot like this girl back then, which felt a bit unsettling. High school had been a horrible time for me, and this girl—with her big brown eyes and skinny frame, with her bleached-out but clearly once-brown hair shaped into that ridiculously asymmetrical bob that tapers around to cover her eyes and hide her face, with the slightly hooked nose and sour countenance—felt uncomfortably familiar. I've felt the girl's eyes on me, sure, dressing me up, probably passing judgment. I remember full well how adults in their forties, to a high school kid, seemed ancient. I realize, with some amusement, that the woman in the other corner would probably do anything to look like I do now, even with my furrowed brows and rapidly loosening jowls. She is seventy or so, I assume, and elegant in appearance, with neatly coiffed silver hair and a neatly pressed, if rumpled, suit. Her cheeks and brow, while liver-marked by age, are smooth— perhaps she's had a little cosmetic assistance. I get it, though. Aging isn't easy. I can't judge someone for trying to take an edge off. I'll probably succumb to getting some work done, too, sooner or later.

If I ever get out of here, that is.

Good God, this is taking forever.

"Someone will come," I say to myself under my breath. "They have to come." I am attempting to talk myself out of a panic attack. Because the truth is, being stuck inside a sealed metal space is, to put it mildly, triggering.

I have to get out of here. We all do.

The girl seems to be focused on calming herself down as well—inhaling deeply, audibly blowing carbon dioxide out— and I can smell the increasing sourness of the air trapped in the elevator with us.

The old woman sits quietly, shifting her eyes between me and the girl, as if she is picking us apart. Fair enough. The girl has that ridiculous outfit and I keep gnawing at my nails.

We continue like this for a while—breathing, knowing, staring. But after a point, something has to give.

For me, that point is about a half hour later, when I am unfortunately reminded of the luxurious latte I allowed myself to indulge in at Le Pain Quotidien a couple of hours before.

"Shit," I say, crossing my legs tightly in an effort to suppress the growing urgency of my bladder.

"What? Are you okay?" the girl asks.

"Yeah, I'm...I..." I grab my vacuous purse and peer inside,

knowing I won't find what I need. "Sorry. This is really embarrassing, but do either of you have a plastic bag or a water bottle or something? I really hate to do this, I just—"

"Do you have to use the bathroom?" the elderly woman asks with a tilt of her head.

I nod, sheepish. "Unfortunately."

"I have a can of Diet Coke," says the girl. "I could just finish it?"

"And then you'll have to go too."

"How about this?" The elderly woman shifts herself off her purse and pulls out a snack-size ziplock bag, dumping the remains of dusty almonds onto the floor. "Here," she says, and I take it.

I am pretty sure the bag isn't going to be big enough for the task at hand, but there isn't much choice. I figure I could pee in shifts, applying the Kegel exercises I now regret not doing more of, and maybe pouring the portions…where? How the hell is this going to work?

The other two women turn to face the wall, granting me a semblance of privacy.

I quickly unbutton my jeans and squat as low as I can, holding the bag up as best as I can.

At first I can't go; performance anxiety is a powerful thing. But my quads are burning. I have no choice.

I close my eyes and try to think of a waterfall. An overflowing faucet. A river.

And…the baggie quickly fills up before my bladder is satisfied. Fuck. Okay. Okay. I can do this, I think. I pray.

"I'm so sorry," I say, half standing to relieve the lactic acid building in my thighs. "Can someone empty this? Quickly."

The two of them exchange wary glances, but the girl takes the bag with an outstretched arm, looking all too aware of the moist heat radiating through the thin plastic as she pinches the zip top closed, looking unsure of what to do next.

"Please!" I implore her, overcome with growing desperation. I can only hold back this stream for so long.

It is like that time when I was pregnant with Sonya, when they had me drink twenty-four ounces of water and then wait an hour while my bladder expanded so much it would press into my pelvic cavity or something like that and thus help somehow with the ultrasound. I wasn't really paying attention when the nurse explained it. It was too much. After some pleading, the nurse said I could use the restroom and release just a little bit if it was really so bad. It was, and I did. But what holy hell to start and then stop and have to lie there on the exam table for Lord knows how long while the nurse smeared gelatinous goop across my stomach and then rubbed the vibrator-shaped transducer back and forth until she could get the images she wanted to appear on the monitor. Joel was so happy, almost giddy, watching our little girl swimming around, but all I could focus on was the fact that if the nurse didn't hurry up, that little baby would not be the first female that Joel would have to help clean piss off of. But honestly, right now to be prone on an exam table in an ob-gyn office would be light-years better than this.

"Here." The girl holds the baggie out to the old woman, who just stares at it, her hand remaining primly on her lap. So the girl rests it on the floor, and fortunately the seal holds as the liquid inside spreads out and the bag sinks into the shape of a beached jellyfish. "Hang on," she says. "Just a second." She reaches into her backpack and pulls out a white soda can with bold red lettering. Diet Coke. The kind I used to guzzle by the caseload when I was in college. *You can't beat the feeling!* I am pretty sure that was the tagline back then. But this feeling I would like to beat. Fast. I am not sure how long I can hold out like this, half squatting, legs crossed, my back pressed into the steel wall in an effort to take some strain off my quads.

The girl pulls the tab and the fizzy echo of the released carbon dioxide briefly reverberates off the walls, as if we were stuck between stations on the radio.

"Here goes," she says and guzzles it down, suppressing a burp. She steps over to me. "Use this."

I take it and, noting the ridiculously small opening on top of the can, adjust myself. I say a silent but not fully effective prayer, and with both massive relief and oppressive shame, it becomes all too clear that while a decent amount of the liquid will make it through that tiny hole, a fair amount will not. Yup. This is a pretty awful feeling, I think as I carefully place the can in the corner, hoping not to spill what actually did make it inside.

"Does anyone have a tissue?" I hold my hands out as far from my face as I can. Like Frankenstein's monster. "This is so gross. I am so sorry."

"You'll need more than a tissue," says the old woman, wrinkling her nose. "Maybe take something from there?" She gestures at my Bloomingdale's bag. "There is a fair amount to clean up."

I sigh. Looking at the small puddle on the floor, I know the old woman is right. I start plucking items out of the bag.

When it is over, when my hands have been dried off with one of the new shirts I just bought, when the floor has been wiped clean with another, when the girl and I have slowly poured the liquid out of the bag, then the can, letting it seep into the crack at the bottom of the door, when we have all awkwardly blushed at this shared humiliation, the girl shakes her head. "I shouldn't have had that soda," she says, resigned, and we start the process all over again. And then, as the sound of rushing liquid tends to inspire things, the older woman pulls herself up and takes a turn, which is an even more cumbersome effort as she needs to have me and the girl support her in her squat lest she fall over and spill the entirety of the bag's contents onto the floor.

The process is, at the very least, an icebreaker. Because if you can watch another person piss into a small ziplock bag or through a small hole in a can and then help to dispose of the contents, I think it's fair to say you've shared an experience you wouldn't be quick to forget. The time for averting eyes is over.

And so, we don't. We catch each other's eyes and offer sympathetic smiles, a nod to the fact that we are, the three of us, fully in this together because, as has now become painfully obvious, there isn't anyone else.

"So that happened," I say ruefully, trying to lighten the mood.

The old woman blows out an exaggerated and knowing sigh. "It most certainly did."

"What did?" asks the girl.

I laugh. "This." I wave my hand at the limp plastic bag by the door, the splatter of urine, and the strong scent of ammonia wafting from my Bloomingdale's shirt.

"Right." The girl tucks her knees up under her school sweatshirt so that again only the toes of her boots stick out.

"Can I ask you something?"

"Whatever," she says, not looking up.

"Why aren't you in school today?" Her presence here does beg this question. Same for all of us. We are all coming or going from somewhere else, right?

"Professional day," the girl mutters and sinks deeper into her sweatshirt. Apparently, this isn't a conversation she wishes to have. It's probably not even true. Schools don't normally have professional days so early in the year, but it's probably not worth pushing the point—it's not as if I am her mother, after all. So I turn to look at the old woman, one eyebrow cocked.

"Doctor's appointment," she says before I can ask.

"Right," I say. "I guess that makes sense."

"What do you mean?" she asks.

"It's just, there are a lot of medical offices around here—"

"It wasn't a urologist, if that's what you're thinking," she says, making what I think is supposed to be a joke. But we don't laugh. Instead, we awkwardly avert our eyes again and shrink into our respective spaces, trying to act as if what had just happened between us a few minutes before had, in fact, not.

4

Morning Edition, Part 2: The Old Woman

October 12
10:30 a.m.
Friendship Heights
The border of Washington, DC and Chevy Chase, MD

The appointment was at 10:30 a.m. and it was fast—faster than a haircut even. There was no drying time, after all, just the nurse putting pressure on the spots of the old woman's forehead where the needle had pricked—a small massage to spread the milligrams of low-potency poisons smoothly under the skin.

"There," the nurse said, standing back to admire her handiwork as if she had just carved a bust out of marble. "That went well. I don't think there should be any bruising." She held out a hand mirror for the patient to see for herself.

The old woman studied her reflection. She knew it would take an hour or two for the treatment to fully kick in, but this was just the first dose and she could already see the lines across her forehead starting to flatten out.

"What do you think?" the nurse asked.

"A flash of my youth," the woman replied, tilting her head this way and that to get a glimpse of how she looked from different angles. Actually, she quickly realized, it wasn't so much her younger self that she was reminded of. With her carefully coiffed white hair and classic pink tweed Chanel-style skirt suit, her professional sleekness resembled that of her mother. Which is what she wanted. Her mother had always looked so stylish and important. Vital. Formidable even. Not the dried-up and withered old lady she was sure her own daughter had seen when they last spoke the week before.

She cringed—as best as her increasingly paralyzed facial muscles would allow—as she recalled their conversation, as she remembered how her daughter had made it so abundantly clear that she didn't think her mother was equipped to continue living alone in that oversized house.

"Mother," her daughter had said, knowing full well that the old woman did not like to be referred to with such formality, that she felt there was something almost infantilizing about it, especially when her daughter used such a pedantic tone. "Mother," her daughter repeated. "You have to face the truth. You're being selfish."

Selfish.

How could staying put in her lifelong home be selfish? she wanted to ask. She had even invited her daughter to move back in with her, if she so desperately wanted to live in the house. How selfish was that? But now that her daughter was locked in on this idea that it was time for her to move out, it really didn't matter what she said. The wheels were in motion. She had to find another way to persuade her daughter to lay off while still keeping a modicum of their relationship intact.

She held the mirror a little further out so her eyes could adjust and wondered what her daughter would make of her now. Maybe she would stop acting as if aging had reduced her mother to incompetent infancy? Or perhaps she was delusional to think that smoothing out her skin could do anything to smooth out her relationship with her daughter.

She placed the mirror on the exam table and slowly rose to her feet.

"Thank you, dear," she said. "It all looks very good."

The nurse took the woman's wool jacket off the hook and held it open wide, just as one might before bundling up a small child. The woman let the nurse wrap her up, accepting this for more than it was; tender gestures were rare in her life. She'd take them where she could.

When she reached the street, the temperature seemed to have dropped, or maybe it was just that she was warm from being inside, but after a few minutes of waiting for a cab, the breeze started to cut like a blade and she decided to take the Metro instead, grateful, at least, that the platform to the elevator provided shelter from the wind.

As she stood there waiting, the teenage girl with the oversized sweatshirt arrived. She stepped directly in front of the woman and began to repeatedly push the down button, even though it was already lit. The woman wanted to admonish her, tell the girl she was wasting her time, but she bit her tongue. What did it matter? The elevator would come when it came.

5

SENSE MEMORY: EMILIA

October 12
12:58 PM
Friendship Heights Metro
Washington, DC

You would think that being trapped in a dark void would be a good place to be if you wanted to ponder difficult things—the fight you had with your husband, what you want to make for dinner, the death of your mother, really anything at all. But honestly, the longer I sit here, the more it feels like I am sitting in the middle of a vacuum, one that is sucking my brain dry of thoughts. It reminds me of the times I have come out of general anesthesia; it feels a little bit like that, like your mind is sort of hovering between here and there.

It isn't until sometime later, Lord only knows how much, that a shift in the odor draws me back to the present space and tense. Cutting through the lingering scent of urine, a slight draft carries a different but all-too-familiar scent in my direction—a weird combination of a frat house bathroom after a big party and the type of excrement one might more routinely find on the bottom of one's shoe.

I know exactly what it is.

"Did someone step on a ginkgo fruit?" I ask, breaking the silence that has been holding steady for quite some time now.

The girl mutters an apology, but that isn't really my point. Mostly I am just trying to make conversation, trying to fill up the time. I grant that this is a pretty weak start, but I prattle on.

"No, no. It's just… Don't you hate them?" I ask. "We used

to have one in front of my house when I was a kid. We would track the pulp into the house and my mother would go nuts, as if we had deliberately soiled her foyer. I had to sweep the walkway multiple times a day, it got so bad. The city wouldn't let us cut the tree down unless we got permission from the majority of our neighbors. It took years. They finally relented after my mother died, mostly because they felt bad for us. I think, honestly, it was probably the nicest thing my mom ever did for me."

Neither of them responds, at least not verbally. There isn't even a shard of light our eyes can adjust to. If they are nodding or smiling or frowning or even sleeping, I wouldn't know. So I keep on talking. "You know, only the female trees bear fruit," I say. "You're supposed to plant the male ones. I guess some urban planner back in the 1920s had issues with gender identity."

No one laughs at my lame joke, but it's fine. I am just looking for distractions from the thoughts that are bothering me more, like how getting stuck in an elevator seems so fitting, how it is what I probably deserve, a twisted kind of punishment for—I could go on. The list is long. Like my selfishness this morning. I shouldn't have burdened Sonya with the anniversary business. I shouldn't have let Joel stomp off under such a black cloud. I definitely shouldn't have gone shopping. It was ridiculous to think there could be any redemption in that. But maybe if I had stopped to talk to the homeless man hawking copies of *Street Sense*, or if, for a moment, I had taken some interest in the world outside of my obsession with this infernal anniversary, and instead of being stuck in my own head I had paused to browse the plastic newspaper boxes that line the entrance to the Metro station, maybe I would have been delayed long enough to miss this particular descent. Maybe those newspaper headlines would have given me something more interesting to think about, something to occupy my thoughts so that this current state of limbo would not be making me feel so, well, in limbo.

I take a deep breath, which is no easy feat, considering. The urine-hinted rotting ginkgo aroma is just the start of it, a loathsome accent added to the now overbearing varieties of scents. Strangely metallic fragrances emanate from the elevator walls, which are textured in an endless expanse of cold little bumps with condensation settling into the grooves. It's almost as if the walls are starting to sweat, giving off a musty, mineral scent that is hard to describe—rather like trying to define the color blue or how long forever is. The air in the elevator is now pungent with body odor, acrid with urine, heavy with sweat, and sour with fear. And with our body heat further warming up the space, the smell is becoming increasingly pronounced. It reminds me of my post-collegiate years in New York City—and I fervently thank God that as of yet it is only liquid forms of nature that have come calling. Although I am feeling a bit queasy. After an hour and change trapped inside of this fetid elevator with two other people and no end in sight, it is becoming increasingly difficult to quiet my guts. I exhale with some exaggeration, eager to move on to non-olfactory details of my current dilemma. I need to focus on a different one of my five senses.

Suddenly, as if to oblige me, the light turns shockingly bright and holds steady.

My eyes take a moment to adjust and then I idly cast my gaze around the small space.

The down arrow of the button panel points to the girl's head like some sort of ominous message, so I follow the direction, ultimately locking eyes with the teenage girl beneath. She is still curled up against her knees, her sweatshirt pulled over her legs, the school logo stretched across the dark-green fabric like a billboard, the tips of her boots still sticking out cartoonishly from under the hem.

"Now, isn't this a coincidence," I say, as if I hadn't already had the thought hours before.

"What?" asks the girl.

"I went there," I say, wagging a finger at her chest.

"What do you mean?"

"Your sweatshirt? Washington Day School? I went there. I had the same one."

"Oh," she says, biting on a cuticle. She doesn't seem to know what to do with this information but offers up that, yes, she's supposed to graduate in the spring. But please don't ask her about college applications, she says, making a millisecond of eye contact with me before shrinking back against the wall.

I nod knowingly. That awkward gesture, that insecure slouch, it is all so familiar. I am sure I know her from somewhere. Hair color, eye color, and height aside, she could almost pass for an older, surlier version of Sonya. With the sharp angles of her shoulders practically framing her ears and her small body engulfed by her extra-large hoodie, she looks fragile and sad, and it breaks my heart a little; I remember exactly how it felt to be a teenage girl feeling like that.

"What's your name?" I ask.

She scowls at me through her darkly lined eyes as if to say *you first*, as if this question were a dare.

"Okay." I relent. "I'm Emilia. And you are...?"

But the older woman answers before the girl can respond, a bemused expression crossing her face. "So am I," she says, with a quick, surprised smile; wrinkles envelop her papery skin in the harsh glare of fluorescent light, like one of those sped-up videos showing cracks rippling across a drought-struck, dusty earth. As her smile recedes, the lines disappear, blurring back into her face as quickly as they came. I briefly avert my eyes. "Emilia," the old woman says, drawing me back. "That's my name too."

"Really?" I say. "That's funny." Because it is. But also, it's not. I glance at her quickly, then over to the girl, and then back. "Emilia? With two i's?"

"Most people call me Millie."

"Well, that's easy then," I say. "Nobody has ever called me Millie." Nor will they, I hope. I can almost smell the mothballs when I say the name. "My husband sometimes calls me Mils, but that's as close as it gets." Actually, if I am being honest, he hasn't been using any diminutives lately; he hasn't in a long while. He used to have scores of nicknames for me. Now it's just Emilia all the time, and often with an exasperated emphasis on the final *a*. Emili-ah. But I don't say that. "Anyway," I say instead, "it's nice to meet you, Millie." I stretch out a hand.

She doesn't take it. "No thank you."

"Right." I drop my arm. Of course. She knows where our hands have been.

"Regardless, it's nice to—"

"That's so weird," the girl pipes up before Millie can finish her reply. "That's my name too."

"Emilia?" Millie and I both ask.

"I mean, sort of," says the girl, sounding more animated than she has been this whole time. "Nobody ever calls me that. Most people call me Em, but it is kind of a nickname. I mean, because—"

"Em?" Millie and I interrupt her in unison, and the girl nods, causing the hood to finally fall back off her head.

"Yes," I say. "That is definitely odd." Em was my nickname when I was a kid. A kid who looked a lot like the one in front of me now. "Millie, were you once an Em too?" I ask the older woman, this Millie. "This is some kind of joke, right?" Because, come on, as much as my gut is starting to tell me one thing, my head is telling me another. All three of us with the same name, all stuck in the same elevator together? What are the chances of that? That would be ridiculous. Beyond ridiculous—it would be totally absurd.

Except that the older woman quickly says yes. Yes, she was. She pushes an errant strand of white hair behind one ear. "And…" She blows out a slow breath. "I was once called Em too. For a short period of time," she says quietly. Her voice is clear, but there is a raspy undertone that suggests she is or was once a smoker, or maybe it's just the gravelly voice of the very old. "When I left for college, I insisted that everyone call me Emilia. Over time it morphed into Millie."

"How come?" I ask.

"That's what my granddaughter called me when she was little. I like it. It reminds me of her."

"This is really weird," says young Em, stating the obvious, except that what is simply weird for Em is quickly becoming, at least for me, more than a little bit disturbing. I don't dare ask for their last names.

The buzzing sound starts up again, interrupting our chatter. It gets louder and louder. The walls are practically vibrating. The fluorescent light flickers for a few seconds, until it stabilizes on a darker setting that casts the elevator in unsettling hues of grayish blue.

I squint, trying to get a better look at them, these Emilias, but even in the strange light I can make out the similarity of their large dark eyes and wide mouths. There's that soft arch of their brows. The sweatshirt. Em's asymmetrical haircut, which is identical to the one I got on Astor Place when I ran away from the pack during my junior class trip to New York.

I shake my head hard, as if trying to flick something off. "No." I blink. I breathe out through my nose. But even the best Pranayama technique can't change what I am seeing. "No way," I say.

The older woman, Millie, appears to be contemplating something similar, judging by the drawn look on her face. After all, she is fully aware of what she has looked like over the years. She must have photos. Videos. Memories. In person, though, in the flesh, this has to be another thing entirely.

It is totally absurd, this situation. It makes no sense. Any time travel I know of is total fiction and this is all too real. But even if that is what is happening here, even if I can forget the fact that the three of us being here together is an affront to the laws of physics, among other things, what even brought each of us here? Literally. What brought us to the Friendship Heights Metro station at 11:15 on a Thursday morning in October? Why are we here? I mean, I know I was shopping and all that, and this Em here says she didn't have school, but really? And Millie? Thirty years into the future? Would the Metro even be a thing? I hate taking the train now and can't imagine why on earth I would be taking it then. And even if she's not me, if this is just some crazy odd coincidence, I really can't imagine why such an elegant-looking old woman would be taking the Metro at all.

As for Em…

No, wait.

I know. Of course I do. If this is real, if she is somehow me, then I know why she is here. And even if she isn't me, given the dysphoric air about her, I don't think I'd be far off in my reasoning.

But before I am quite ready to articulate anything out loud, before I can ask them some clarifying questions, the light flickers a few more times, there is a loud clunking sound in the distance, the straining of gears, and once again everything goes black.

6

Morning Edition, Part 3: Em

October 12, 1987
7:30 a.m.
Upper Northwest
Washington, DC

Earlier in the day, Em had in fact gotten ready to go to school.
That had been her intention, anyway. The large blue digits on
her boxy clock radio flipped to 7:30 and WHFS blasted out a
chipper refrain from Elvis Costello about how he writes a book
every day. Every day. Whatever. She smacked the snooze bar
to shut it down, only to be woken ten minutes later as Cyndi
Lauper crooned on about waiting for a change of heart. She
shoved the radio off the bedside table and it hit the floor, causing a small crack on one corner and the music to devolve into
static. Sighing, she got up and pulled the plug out of the wall.
She brushed her teeth, rimmed her eyes with thick black kohl,
rubbed concealer into the scar above her eyebrow, and shaped
her bangs with some generously applied gel. Leaning forward
over the sink, she inspected her skin, restraining herself from
popping a small zit that was emerging in the crease by her nose.

It was almost 8:15 by the time Em laced up her black Doc
Martens boots and stomped downstairs—although if pushed
there was no way she could account for why it had taken her so
long to do so little.

"Honey," her dad said as she entered the kitchen, "you're
going to be late." He handed her a cup of coffee.

Em took it. She held the cup up to see what it said. They
had a collection of decorated coffee mugs, and her father often

curated them with whatever daily affirmation he wanted to impart, since actually having a conversation with his teenage daughter had become challenging at best. Usually the mugs had cute Sandra Boynton cartoons with cheerful images of animals prancing and saying anthropomorphically "punny" things like "Isle of Ewe" and "Udder Cool," or they had fancy text with inspirational aphorisms ("I am not afraid of storms, for I am learning to sail my ship."—L.M. Alcott), and some had goofy pop-culture catchphrases ("Where's the Beef?"). The father knew, however, that this day was going to be a hard one for Em and any of those would have been inappropriate. Instead, he had given her a mug with red, orange, and yellow stripes that clashed with the neon-green polish that was chipping off her fingernails. On top of the background were black silhouettes of three little birds flying around the Bob Marley lyrics about not needing to worry about anything circling the mug in an overly loopy script.

It did not have the desired effect.

"You have got to be kidding me," Em spat out. She poured the coffee down the drain and tossed the mug into the sink as if it were toxic, breaking the handle in half.

"Honey." Her father reached for her shoulder, but she swatted him off. "I'm trying," he said wearily.

"It shouldn't be that hard, Dad. Just tell the truth."

"I have told the truth. You know that."

"No, Dad. I don't know that."

This was the crux of the argument that had been going on for a year now, the question of how exactly her mother had died and who was responsible, and it is the reason why, at that moment, on the first anniversary of that horrible day, Em decided that standing in the kitchen with him was most definitely not where she wanted to be.

She grabbed her Sony Walkman off the counter, slung her bulging backpack over one shoulder, grabbed her keys off the hook, and stormed out the door, not caring that the stinking ginkgo berries squished underfoot as she made her way, in a fury, to the street.

Her neighborhood was full of them; female ginkgo trees peppered her entire block. In a few weeks' time, the vomit-like stench from their dropping fruit would permeate the streets.

Em found them relentless, these trees. She had recently done a research paper on ginkgoes for her biology class and was horrified to discover that they can live to be thousands of years old, occasionally even shooting weird nubby roots from their branches that created reinforcement after a traumatic event. *Basal chichi*, they were called. A ridiculous name for a ridiculous tree with ridiculous fruit, and to Em the offensive odor the trees created was a fitting scent for the day, a kind of olfactory background music, and the crush of the berries underfoot was oddly satisfying, not unlike a well-popped pimple.

And this in turn helps to explain why, a handful of hours later in the day when she has been stuck in a Metro elevator for more minutes than she cares to count, the yellowed pulp of the ginkgo fruit remains stuck in the creviced soles of her boots, emitting a putrid scent that only people deeply familiar with the female ginkgo tree could accurately assess.

7

Naming Conventions: Emilia

October 12
1:27 p.m.
Friendship Heights Metro
Washington, DC

It's not easy to get comfortable in this place, but I figure that at least in the dark I can have a few minutes to myself, maybe grab control of my tangled mess of thoughts and straighten them out. *This is impossible. This is impossible.* The words repeat in a loop, like a record skipping or a fully unproductive meditative mantra. Om Namah, my ass. This is impossible.

But what if it's not?

What if, in fact, the impossible is possible? If it is true? Then what? Is this an opportunity or just some sort of cruel joke? And if it is true, then what could I possibly say to myself at seventeen? To Em? What would I want to know at that point in my life? That everything is going to be fine? That life will become a series of unicorn rides and fairytale balls? Please. And Millie? What on earth would I say to her? What would she want to say to me? It's a fantasy everyone has, I assume. Don't we all think we want to know what will happen in our lives? I obsess about it all the time. What will happen to me, to the people I love? But faced with the possibility of actually finding out—I don't know, will Sonya end up happy? Will I win the lottery? Will I stay healthy, what will the world even be like decades from now?—honestly, I have no idea what I want to ask, what I want to be revealed. What if I don't like the answers? It's making me feel queasy just thinking about it.

My head is starting to hurt.

After a number of impatient minutes, I lean back against the elevator wall, relishing the coolness of the metal through my thin sweater. I feel as if I am overheating from the inside out, at the tail end of a perimenopausal hot flash. I strip down to my thin camisole top. My cheeks feel flushed and a line of sweat is rapidly moistening my hairline.

I lean back again.

This feels good. For a moment. Then, this hard space lost in time suddenly becomes vividly real, even if I can't presently see any of it. In fact, it's not entirely unfamiliar. In a way, I have been here before. Not literally stuck in an elevator with two versions of myself, of course not. But this is not the first time I've experienced something that seems too absurd to be real, too out of place—something that makes me briefly question my own sanity before finally setting it straight.

Like the time I saw a furry red panda jet across our lawn. I knew—thanks to Sonya's obsession with the stuffed version she got at the National Zoo a few years ago, complete with an accompanying booklet—that such mammals were native to Asia and had no place in Northwest DC. No place except the zoo, of course, which was about a mile and a half away from our house and, I found out later that evening, was exactly where the creature had sprung from, so I wasn't crazy at all. Or that time when I thought I saw my long-dead mother picking through a stack of apples at the supermarket. Was I losing my mind? But it wasn't my mother. First off, my mother would never have been caught *alive* in the supermarket, much less dead. It was just some wannabe socialite dressed way too nicely for the produce aisle. I blamed the mistake on dried-out contact lenses and an insufficient intake of caffeine.

But this?

No. This is too much. Short of this being a dream—but, really, who has dreams so lucid and so long?—there is no way to explain it. There is no way that this slight teenage girl with the asymmetrical highlighted hair and extra-large Washington

Day School sweatshirt could possibly be me. Or that this older woman… I mean, come on! As if in some thirty-odd years I'll throw in the towel and let the grays win out? Or that I'll be so…so…what? Fossilized? Is that what I will be like? How can this even be real? How can it be that we are all really one and the same? But I have to concede that maybe the answer is just simply that it can be, and it is.

I am not the only one trying to think this through.

"I can't believe we all have the same name," says Em.

Again with the obvious, although I do have to agree. I was also called Em once, that is true. But Millie? Millie. I repeat the name a few times in my head. No. No way. It's definitely not time for that yet. It's just a weird coincidence. The name, their features. Maybe that is all it is.

Millie starts to rationalize in a similar way. "I've seen some strange things in my time," she says, in a manner which is suggestive of a shoulder shrug. "Sometimes," she says wistfully, "it feels as if life is just a string of one inexplicable situation after the next."

"Like what?" I ask, eager to normalize this increasingly bizarre situation.

"Well," says Millie. She pauses while we wait to hear what sort of explanation-defying events she can conjure up. "I know," she says. "Like Donald Trump igniting an insurrection in the middle of a global pandemic? When that was happening, I was—"

"Wait. What are you talking about?" I ask, because regardless of whatever personal anecdote she is about to impart, my understanding is that Donald Trump's first term in office has only just begun and the only pandemic I am familiar with is our country's brush with Ebola several years ago. Horrified, I realize I may have to accept that Millie might in fact know a thing or two about the future. And if she does… I briefly close my eyes, inhale loudly, and then release my breath. "Are you saying that Donald Trump—"

"Donald Trump?" Em interrupts, confused. "You mean the guy married to that Ivana woman?"

I am about to correct this information, tell her that it's Melania now, when it occurs to me that the answer to one simple question might clarify everything all at once. "What year do you each think it is?"

Em and Millie each take a pause and then, at the exact same time, they say "1987" and "2047."

"What do you mean?" I ask. "It's 2017."

This makes absolutely no sense. But "yes, it is" and "no, it's not" only goes so far as we each try to argue the point.

Millie emits a small laugh under her breath, as if this is some kind of inside joke, which maybe it is. Then she says, very matter-of-factly, "Perhaps it's all three."

"This is so crazy!" I bury my face in my hands, hoping that when I remove them a different reality will prevail.

But no, it is still as pitch dark as the interior cabin of a wrecked ship long settled on the ocean floor. I can hear the faint movements of the other two and smell the sour muskiness of our bodies packed in this small, stifled space. I am most definitely not alone.

"So we are all one and the same?" I ask, hysteria tingeing my voice, my heart beating at such a furious pace that I can feel it in my throat. I inhale deeply in an attempt to steady my nerves. "Am I supposed to believe that we've somehow crossed space and time and landed in the same place? In here?"

"That does seem to be the case," Millie calmly replies. "Although I'd argue we didn't really cross space. We all got on at Friendship Heights, did we not?"

"But this"—I wave my hands around, but again, the communication implied by the gesture is to the benefit of no one—"this is impossible."

"Apparently, it's not," Em mutters.

"I'd have to agree," says Millie.

We sit with this for a moment until young Em breaks the silence. "It's like that play," she says. "All of us stuck in here like this, you know?"

I do not know.

Millie says she thinks she might. "Yes. Yes. What was the writer's name again, dear? I don't recall."

"Sartre," Em says, encouraged.

"Yes," says Millie. "That's right."

"What play?" I demand.

"*No Exit,*" Em says, exasperated, like I should know it. "I read it last year."

"Yes," says Millie. "I remember it. I saw a production not too long ago. What was that famous line? 'Hell is other people.' Isn't that it?"

"Yeah. That's right," says Em. "Although I guess we just established that maybe it's possible we aren't other people."

"Fair enough," Millie says, briefly ruminating on the point. "Maybe this is our own personal hell, in that case. It is worth considering."

"That's ridiculous," I say. "It was just a play."

"You'd be happy to know I got an A on the final exam."

"Lot of good that does now," I say. "What was it about, again? Three people stuck in a room, right?"

"Which is hell," says Em, a touch too enthusiastically. She is enjoying herself more than one might expect of a teenager trapped in a steel box in the pitch dark, hovering who knows how many feet in the air. "They're in hell. Each of them has done something horrible in life. But instead of the devil or his henchmen, they torment each other. They drive each other mad."

"'Hell is other people,'" Millie says, repeating the one line of the script I do remember now.

There is a sudden loud buzzing sound and the light flickers back on just enough that I can make out Millie and Em's shadowy contours.

Millie's patent leather purse rests neatly on top of her carefully folded coat, a stark comparison to my side of the elevator—my shopping bags are piled up around me in a disorderly heap, with clothes draped on top and shoved in between them. In the murky light, it probably looks as if I am reclining in an overstuffed chair. Em, however, is still balled up under the tent of her heavy sweatshirt, hugging her knees.

"Aren't you hot?" I ask, surprising myself that of all the questions to ask, this is the one that comes out.

"I'm fine," says Em.

Her eyes track over me. There's nothing to be ashamed of, I suppose. Let her look. People often tell me I look good for my age. Not just my face, but my figure too. My arms are thin but defined. I wish I could say that's because I work out a lot, but honestly it's more a matter of lucky genetics. My mom had arms like this too.

Either way, I doubt Em has ever really thought about what she might look like far in the future. Why would she? If memory serves—if I accept that she is me—then lately she hasn't even wanted to think about the following month. Or day. She hasn't been sure she would even get there. But here she is, looking at me, this older Emilia, trying to understand that if I am her, if that is at all possible, then she is seeing what she will look like in middle age; she is seeing that one day she will *be* middle-aged, just as I am now. That has to be unsettling, but oddly, it doesn't appear to be terrifying, judging by Em's calm expression. She can see that we both have lush eyelashes, and our brows could give Brooke Shields a run for her money, which can be a good thing or a bad thing, depending on the decade. She can also see the deep, angry-looking crease between my brows and the crescent-shaped grooves extending from the outer sides of my nose to the edges of my mouth. But like her, my lips are full, and my eyes are wide. I don't look all that bad, for someone as old as her mom. As old as her mom—my mom—would have been, anyway. Had she lived.

I tuck up my legs, rest my head against my knees, and stare at the floor in an effort to suppress a rising tide of nausea.

"I'm pretty certain this isn't a play," Millie says.

"It's a good thing that it's not that play," says Em.

"Why is that a good thing?" I ask.

"You want this to be hell? For real?"

"I certainly don't," Millie answers for me. "But then again, maybe this is it. Maybe my damnation is having to deal with myself for eternity. Marinate in my own misery."

I concede that would be awful…and that it probably fits. I certainly don't have another explanation.

"Nah," says Em, who, to be frank, hasn't had to live with herself as long as I have. Or as long as Millie has, for that matter. "It's not like that. This isn't the same hell as in the play, anyway."

"Clearly, it's not exactly the same," Millie says. "In the play, the characters are set up—"

"Wait!" It's all too much. Enough about the stupid play. I need a minute to think. I take a deep breath. There is something incomprehensible at play here. And then it hits me—there is one fact that can clarify our commonality more than anything else, come heaven or hell.

"Tell me," I ask with some deliberation. "Each of you. Where were you on October 12, 1986?"

The light flickers, and it becomes horrifically bright.

I blink and rub my eyes as they adjust to the light. Looking across at Millie and Em, I can acknowledge that the resemblance between the three of us is uncanny. More than uncanny.

I say it again. "October 12…?"

"Like, a year ago?" asks Em, eyes shifting from my face to the floor.

I shake my head dismissively. "It was thirty-one years ago." I point at Millie. "October 12, 1986. Where were you?" My heart is racing so fast it is almost difficult to speak. "It was Columbus Day weekend. Late morning. On the Eastern Shore?"

"I think you know exactly where I was," says Millie.

"And you, Em?" I ask. "Where were you?"

The girl doesn't answer. She just shakes her head and collapses into her corner, and then the light snaps back to total blackness.

"So…" she says. "This is fucked up." It is the last thing anyone says for some time.

8

Darkness Visible: Emilia

October 12
2:26 p.m.
Friendship Heights Metro
Washington, DC

This dark is now so dark it is almost incomprehensible. It must be just like this inside a black hole. Who even knew that such darkness was possible? I sure as hell didn't. I try closing my eyes and then blink a few times, thinking this action could somehow change things.

It doesn't.

I can't see them, but Millie and Em are close enough for me to feel their radiating body heat. I draw in a long, deep breath, and I can hear them doing the same. Which makes sense, I guess; chances are good that we are all thinking similarly contorted thoughts, reaching for the tangible facts of that long-ago afternoon, that devastating day when my mother died, because the truth itself feels too mercurial. Or maybe not the truth, exactly. Memories. Yes. I almost say it aloud. Memories. That memory. I should start with that.

"I guess this is more interesting than yet another trip to the Eastern Shore," I say, loudly enough to be sure they can hear me.

Neither of them replies.

I sigh, mostly for effect. "Whatever you were doing before you stepped in here, it had something to do with today being the day that it is, right?"

Silence.

I carry on. "Fine. That's my story, anyway. Retail therapy to remember my mother. That's what I was doing before this happened." I laugh. "She'd probably approve."

I might not be able to see Em nodding, fighting off the curl of her lip, but I know that she is. I know Millie is too. Or even if she's not nodding, her silence is an acknowledgment of sorts. She's not arguing me down.

Which is a start.

"Actually," I continue. "Mom would probably have a thing or two to say about what I bought, right? Not tailored enough? Too casual? Maybe even too young for my age, right? You probably wouldn't want to be caught dead in this stuff, Em. But still."

I keep on chattering and the other two keep on not responding. They are still here, though. I can hear Millie shifting around, the rustle of fabric as she crosses and uncrosses her legs. I can smell the faint vanilla scent of the hair gel Em uses to keep that curtain of bangs arranged across her face. Tenax—that's what it was called. It was like glue. She may as well have used Shellac. I know I shouldn't reach out to touch her hair, but man, do I want to. I want to feel that crunchy texture; I remember pulling a strand in front of my eyes and twisting it around, the dried gel flaking off like dandruff. I used to visit Rodman's Market with Amy, looking for the green aluminum tubes of Tenax, and we'd harangue the manager whenever they didn't have it in stock.

"It's funny," I say to Em. "I can hardly remember what Friendship Heights looked like back when I was your age. It keeps morphing in my mind. I mean, Bloomingdale's only opened a few years ago. What was the name of the store that used to be there? Hecht's? It's like boiling a frog in water, you don't notice as the temperature slowly rises, right? Or as things slowly change. What was across the street from Hecht's? I can't remember."

As I keep talking into the silence, it dawns on me that if I want to engage Em and Millie, I probably need to be more direct. I need to just go there, to the heart of the memory I am sure none of us want to talk about but that I am also quite sure none of us can shake. Because the truth is, this is not the first time I've been stuck like this, when time has collapsed in on me. And surely, then, they have been there too.

"You know what?" I say to my taciturn audience. "In a way, we've been trapped like this before. It almost makes sense."

"What?" Em asks. Her tone is snappish, but I smile. At least the conversation is finally less unipolar.

"Em," I say. "So weird to call you that. Anyway, yes. You both know perfectly well where we were thirty-one years ago, or one year ago, whatever, but at pretty much this time of day. Maybe a few hours earlier, right? Like, around the time we all stepped into this elevator? We need to talk about that."

"Oh dear God," says Millie.

"Jesus Christ," Em spits out. At almost the exact moment of Em's exclamation, the elevator gives a big shake, as if she's invoked it.

There is a sudden jolt, a short drop, and my stomach lurches toward my chest, the way it used to when Sonya and I would challenge each other to fly higher and higher on the tree swing in the backyard—a feeling of sudden, plummeting descent.

And then, abruptly, the elevator shudders to a stop.

Everything is still.

"Are you guys okay?" I ask once I remember to breathe.

Millie lets out a short groan but insists that she is fine. "It is a good thing I was already sitting down," she acknowledges ruefully.

"Em?" I ask. "Em, are you okay?"

Em emits a deep, almost guttural wail, followed by a shriek so loud my ears start to ring.

"It's fine, dear," Millie says, trying to calm her down. "We will be fine. Just…just…"

"Just what?" Em spits back. "Just sit here until we rot? Just sit here chitchatting in the dark like this is fucking normal? This is not fucking normal!"

Neither Millie nor I say anything after that. No point in arguing the hard truth.

"Do you think this is a fucking joke?" Em goes on, clearly emboldened by her use of profanities—the forbidden fruit of cursing in front of adults still carries a charge. "You think that being trapped in here is like some kind of fucking reunion? You can count me out. I'm not interested in bonding with you about what happened that day. This is bullshit."

I am not surprised by her response, knowing as I do how awful it feels to scratch at this memory. I, too, would rather keep it down, below the surface. I've been doing it for years. But here we are, and clearly we have to face some facts.

The first fact is obvious. My mother—the eternally revered Sally Fletcher—is Em's mother and Millie's too. And it is indisputable that Sally Fletcher died tragically on October 12, 1986, at approximately 11:17 a.m.

Those facts are unalterable.

What I question is why it happened at all.

That is the heart of the conflict that has overshadowed my life. And Em's (at least for the past year). And I am guessing Millie's too. Why did our mother have to die? And, more fundamentally, was it our fault? Well, we know it was our fault, but what we are supposed to do with that information is another question entirely.

"Come on," I say. "We are going to have to talk about it at some point."

Em responds by spitting out a few more delicious curses like "Fuck that!" and "This is bullshit!"

"Millie, how about it? Can we please go there?" I ask, and finally Millie concedes. She knows, we all know, that if we are going to find a way to end this nightmare, we need to start at a moment when our memory is definitively shared.

We need to start inside a different metal box that had also once brought us precariously close to oblivion.

PART II

9

A Wrinkle in Timelines: Em

October 12, 1986
11:17 a.m.
Bay Breeze, MD

It was overcast and the afternoon light flattened the road. The only thing that stood in relief was the steam coming off the asphalt, which had been darkened by the rain that was only starting to lift. Em was driving, her first time at the wheel on a wet public road. She remembers the road signs flying by, her desperate effort to focus on the road, on the curves, always fearfully mindful of the drop to her right and the waves crashing on the rocky shore far below. She recalls her father grasping the strap on the passenger side, trying to remain calm, her mother thrusting herself between the seats, telling Em what to do, how to do it, and that she was doing it all wrong.

Em remembers her white-knuckled grip on the wheel, her gaze locked on the road ahead. It was supposed to be a treat, her driving the new car before the ink on her permit had a chance to dry, a prize to make the horror of the previous day disappear, to alleviate the tension of the fight they'd had that morning. But her mother's incessant nagging and her father's attempt to contain it had evolved from an irritating buzz into a shitstorm of parental snaps.

Em tried to remain calm and to ignore her expanding headache, to keep her eyes on the road and her foot gingerly on the pedal while her mother barked from the back, lobbing instructions that felt more like insults.

"Don't pump the pedal like that! Be sure to check the side

mirrors! Speed up!" she admonished. When she shouted, "Slow down!" for the third time, Em had had enough. Em turned her head to snap back.

That part of the memory feels distant, but everything from that moment forward always happens in present tense. The experience is eternally fresh, as easily accessed as a book on a shelf. Pull it out, blow off the dust, and there it is. The story of the moment when everything changed.

The car veers off the road, the force of impact splintering the railing. Then time slows. Within five seconds, maybe ten, the car teeters forward, careening over the edge and into the bay—each of those seconds a seeming eternity filled with its own colors, chaos, and noise.

It is exactly as one might imagine. Metal screeching on metal at 50 miles an hour. An explosion of sound that is simultaneously a deep bass and a piercingly high pitch. It feels almost as if the noise itself might be the cause of the impact. A sonic boom. The breaking of the sound barrier.

The sheer volume of noise, followed by its complete absence, as if all sound were being forcefully sucked out of the world—that is Em's clearest memory of all, that sound shift that occurs just after her body slams hard against the door. Her head hits the window frame so hard her skin splits above her eye. Adrenaline kicks in and she is briefly weightless before the water's surface magnifies in the windshield; it is as if she were looking through a zoom lens on a camera.

The car nosedives into the water and, for a moment, it is quiet and calm. The car bobs like a boat in a storm, her father is shouting to roll down the window before they go under, to unbuckle their seat belts. Stunned, Em is frozen; then, as if jolted by lightning, the cold water cascading inside the car, she springs into action, pushing the button to open the window. The hood of the car is now submerged and the water, halfway up the windshield, pours in faster and faster as her window rolls down.

The latch of the seat belt opens easily, but the seat belt straps feel like the tentacles of an octopus holding her tight, and as the water begins to rise to her shoulders, she is sure she will never get out.

But her father tugs at the straps and she is free. Em pulls herself out the window, lungs ready to burst. The light at the surface is visible and she sets out for it, praying that her desperate need to draw a breath won't betray her. Her arms pull up and back, up and back, the strongest breaststroke of her life, her feet kicking so hard and fast one of her sneakers falls off, something she won't even realize for a good half hour after. Finally, she breaks through, fingers first, launching herself into the air, gasping, heaving, flailing. She spins around, looking, praying, and after an eternity her father's head emerges from the depths.

She screams for him and he screams for her. They are together. Panting too hard to say anything more. For a few moments they wait, staring at the water, waiting for another head to break the surface.

Nothing.

It is cold.

They are chattering, shaking, frantic. Their eyes lock. They know they have to dive back down.

Em pulls against the water, but it's too murky and too deep and she cannot find the car. Lungs on fire, she turns for the surface and breaks through, gasping for air. Her father comes up and dives back down, a few yards away. Again and again, he dives, until his lips are blue and his teeth are chattering, his eyes wide and frightened as they both come to grasp this unspeakable truth. There is nothing to do. They are both too weak and too cold and too shocked to go back.

They leave her mother there, trapped underneath.

Here there is a break in Em's memory. She just remembers sitting in the back of an ambulance, wrapped up like a burrito in a scratchy gray woolen blanket as her father talks to a police officer. Her mother's body lies in one of the myriad ambulances.

"I don't know what happened," her father is saying. "The car just spun out of control."

The officer asks if he has been drinking, as if he might be the one to blame for losing control of the car.

He says no, because he wasn't. But what her father doesn't say, and what he won't ever let Em say, is that he wasn't the one behind the wheel.

Instead he says, muttering repeatedly, "I just lost control. The car accelerated so fast. I don't know what happened. I just lost control."

Em wants to protest but she can't form the words. Her teeth are chattering so hard it sounds like drills are operating inside her head, but through the reverberating noise she hears her father say it again and again, like a record skipping. "I just lost control. I have no idea how that happened. I lost control." He says it so many times that Em almost starts to believe him.

Almost.

10

The Sound of Silence: Emilia

October 12
3:19 p.m.
Friendship Heights Metro
Washington, DC

"It is probably quite nice out by now," Millie says after a long stretch of silence. "It was rather windy this morning, but the forecast looked promising."

"You want to talk about the weather?" I ask.

"To be honest, I wouldn't mind imagining for a moment that we are someplace else."

It's a fair point. The elevator lights are still flickering between darkness and blinding white and the scents of ammonia and steel and body heat have been marinating together to create an altogether unique stew. "Yeah," I say. "There are definitely better places for us to be."

"Together?" Em asks.

"Aren't we always, dear?"

"Ha, ha," I say. But together or not, it would definitely be nice not to be in here. To be outside. The city streets are probably basking in the golden glow of the autumn afternoon, the birds chirping away as they prepare for their southbound journey, a gentle breeze tossing leaves over the sidewalks, later to be gleefully kicked around by laughing children making their way home from school.

I wonder where Sonya is at this moment, how her day is going. Did she make it through to the end of the school day, or did she wind up in the nurse's office with a headache again?

Given our morning, the latter seems more likely. But what if the nurse tried to reach me? I wonder, and I feel crushed, not exactly with guilt but more by something akin to shame. The therapist keeps saying that I'm not present enough. And what mother doesn't pick up when there is a call from the school? Any other mother would be there as fast as she could. Situational obstacles notwithstanding, I can already feel the heavy judgment from our upcoming counseling session. Joel will sit on that shitty brown faux-suede couch, feeling all fucking victorious that he was the one the nurse finally managed to reach.

"Anyplace would be better than this," Em says, and without so much as asking she reaches over and plucks my phone out of my purse. The blue light illuminates the bug-eyed fascination spreading across her face. I am not sure I want to know what she sees, but I ask anyway.

"What time does it say?"

Em holds the phone out so I can see for myself.

3:19 p.m.

Normally at this hour I would be looking out the kitchen window and sipping green tea as I call Sonya to make sure she is on her way home. And Em, she would probably be packing up her locker about now, shoving her textbooks into her backpack, tugging on the stubborn zipper so she can just pack up and get out of there before she has to make insipid small talk with anyone else. At least, that's how I ended each and every day that year, as best as I can recall.

Millie, though—I have no idea how she spends her days. So I ask her, and she says that at 3:19 p.m. she is usually sitting in her sunroom, absorbed in a book, reading glasses resting near the tip of her nose, her small beige-and-white rescue dog, Gigi, curled up at her feet. Instead, she is here in the elevator, looking back at herself...as a teenager and in middle age. "I don't need glasses to bring that sight into any more focus," she says with a laugh. "It pains me enough to look at myself today. Every wrinkle seems like a reminder of some witless mistake."

God, how many times has Millie chastised us in her mind? How many running arguments has she had with us about why we chose this instead of that? How many times has she wanted to comfort us, scold us, do what she had to do to just make it better, to make the pain of growing up go away—and, most importantly, to guide us to make better choices? The part of my brain that stores my own regrets is already filled to capacity. I can't even imagine the overflow another thirty years of living might produce.

But even though we are sitting here now, face to face, I have to wonder if there is anything at all she could change, that any of us can. Anything critical, anyway. Because in our case, the case of Emilia Louise Fletcher, a.k.a. Em, a.k.a. Millie, a.k.a. me, at first blush it's arguably too late. The worst decision of our life has already been made; there's no undoing it. Unless there is another trippy elevator ride in the future that transports us further into the past, all that any of us can do is help each other struggle through the present moment. It is highly unlikely, given the timing of our current predicament, the exact date on which our fates and lives collide, that there is anything else to do but scratch at that fateful moment and force ourselves to spend this agonizing anniversary grappling with our mother's death in a way none of us could have ever imagined.

Millie looks like she wants me to say something, but I am not sure what. I glance at Em, who scowls in response as if I have just said something deeply off-putting. Her thickly kohled eyes look narrowed and mean behind the curtain of her unruly bangs. It's all a mask. I know that. I know that the wall she appears to have built is a thick fog that can be wiped away with a pinkie finger. I know not to take her posturing too seriously. I know she is insecure and vulnerable, and I know just what buttons to push.

"What?" Em demands as I measure her up and down.

"It's nothing. It's just—" I start to say.

"—just that if, in fact, we are all one and the same," Millie interjects, finishing my thought, "and apparently we are, then this is something we've all wished for." She makes a point of making eye contact with both me and Em. "Somehow, we, together, have conjured this up."

"I see that I never get over my habit of interrupting people," I say, narrowing my eyes. "That isn't what I was trying to say."

"Wasn't it though?" Millie says and turns to sulky Em, dismissing my protest.

"Fine," I concede, tucking a strand of hair behind my ear. She isn't right. But she's not wrong either. "Sure. Whatever. We all want to look back and impart words of wisdom, give comfort and so forth. Yada, yada, yada."

"Fat chance of that," says Em. She leans against the handrail and crosses her arms tightly across her chest.

"Fat chance of what, dear?" Millie says, resting a hand on the floor as if to steady herself. I can see the blue veins pulsing beneath her skin, her arthritic fingers conspicuously absent of rings. I tuck my own hands into my lap.

Em turns to me. I raise an eyebrow. "Yes, Em. How about it? Fat chance of what?"

"Of this"—she points her chin at each of us—"being at all comforting. I mean, like, look at you both. God. Look at me." Em cups her chin and sarcastically bats her mascara-coated lashes. "I mean, does this look like a face you can comfort?"

"What's that supposed to mean?" I ask.

"You know what it means."

I can feel myself deflating. Because I do know. I remember that rigidly negative adolescent mind of mine. Cognitive behavioral therapy was in its infancy back then, but I remember those dismal thought spirals and how hard it was to see my way out of them. And, to be completely honest, I know it must be horrifying for Em to see herself middle-aged and old. Not much comfort in that.

I look over at Millie to test myself, to see if I have the stomach to size up my own future self. Unlike Em, imagining myself in old age is a practice I have indulged in quite a bit. So when I realize that Millie, with her elegant suit and sophisticated bob, has held up pretty well, all things considered, it is a small measure of relief.

I am sure none of this offers even a modicum of comfort to Em, though. Graceful aging doesn't erase the fact that the Em of the elevator is already the Em of the terrible mistake. That's not something either Millie or I can help her undo and the repercussions of that fact are written across all of our faces, expensive lotions and potions and Botox notwithstanding.

"I do remember being you," I say, turning back to face Em. "I remember those years. I remember how bad things felt back then…I mean right now. For you. Right now, for you. Maybe that's why we're here. For perspective."

"Kettle, pot, my dear," Millie says before Em can reply. "If I recall correctly, Emilia," Millie continues, "you could still use some guidance yourself at this time in your life."

"Oh, really? So you finally have it all figured out?" I can't hold back my snappish tone. I mean, talk about a trigger. "Everything's a bed of roses for you now, is it?"

"That actually is what I am saying," Millie says softly. "Not that it is a bed of roses, but it does get better. I wish I had understood that sooner. Maybe I would have done things differently. You may think that your life has to be an eternal cycle of penance, but does it ever occur to you that in the end it doesn't have to be? That things might turn out okay?"

"How the fuck can it be okay?" Em explodes. "We killed our mother, for Christ's sake! And nobody believes us!"

Millie laboriously pulls herself up to stand and walks the few steps it takes to reach Em. Gently, she places her spotted hands on the girl's bony shoulder. "Calm down, dear. I know it's still fresh for you, but let's try to talk this through."

Em flinches before Millie makes contact.

"Don't touch me!" She slaps Millie's hands off her shoulders and then spins around, turning her back to us and collapsing

into the corner. She is so done talking it through. I get it. She's
had a year of nonstop talking it through with nobody actually
listening.

Millie looks to me, eyes wide as if she is asking for guidance.

I shake my head. "It's still raw for her," I say. "You and I, at
least we have the benefit of time."

That word—time—sets Em off again. "We shouldn't have
time!" she shouts into the sweaty metal wall. "We shouldn't be
here at all!"

"That is true," I say slowly, striving for the calm but affirm-
ing tone a number of therapists have used on me over the years.
"It is a rather bizarre situation being in this elevator, I will grant
you that."

"No! Not here!" Em turns around. Her nose is wet and
her eyes are raw, and the black eyeliner is starting to spread
raccoon-like around the sockets of her eyes. "We shouldn't be
here! We should be the ones at the bottom of that bay. We
should be down *there*, not in *here*!"

I know this is what she believes, and I know she believes it
deeply. And as much as I would prefer not to, I remember what
it felt like to have those thoughts, to harbor that conviction. I
don't know what to say. Because to be honest, she's not wrong.

Millie, thankfully, does what I usually do in uncomfortable
moments like this. She makes a stupid joke.

"As if this place is such luxury?" she says with an exaggerated sigh. "You know, dear, I realized a long time ago that you
can't have survivor's guilt when it was your fault to begin with.
Flat-out guilt, sure. But that particular flavor of the *it should have
been me* thing gets rather tiresome."

At this, Em shuts her eyes. She doesn't cry though. She
hasn't allowed herself to cry this entire year. I remember that
well, how the teachers and therapists all glommed on to that
fact. While the tears refuse to come, that doesn't mean the pressure doesn't build. Em cups her hands over her eyes and she
screams, the sound reverberating off the walls.

"It's okay, let it out." Millie reaches out to touch Em but

thinks better of it. She looks at me, but I just shake my head. The truth is, I haven't ever had a good cry. Not about my mother, anyway. Not since the day of the accident. Other things, sure, lots of times, but never about that. I refuse to indulge myself with that. Em is no different. She's just as quick to change the topic as I have been for most of my life.

"Wait!" Em says, revealing her face and looking around like an anxious puppy. "Do you hear that?"

I do. I hear it. There's some kind of noise coming from outside.

"Is someone there?"

"Shh. Hang on."

And we all listen hard for whatever, whoever it might be.

There is nothing for a few painful seconds until we hear it again. It's a creak or a mumble. Human or machine. It's impossible to tell, but we jump up and shout at the top of our lungs, hoping against hope that there still might somehow be someone out there, someone who might be able to help.

11

October 12
3:27 p.m.
Friendship Heights Metro
Washington, DC

There isn't.

We wait and we wait, but the sound doesn't return. There's nothing—no one but the three of us. Our throats are raw and we are depleted, stuck in this fucking box with the last people on earth any of us want to be with.

Millie sighs heavily. "So what should we do now? Em, what would—"

"Just leave me alone!" Em shouts into the wall and the words mockingly echo her. *Alone. Alone.* Em slaps the wall hard, repeatedly. "Fuck!" She says it almost rhythmically. "Fuck! Fuck! Fuck! Fuck!" Dropping her arms, she sinks, sniffling, back down to the linoleum floor. She wipes her nose on her sleeve.

Millie fishes through her purse. "Here." She moves closer and holds out a wrinkled handkerchief. Em snatches it, and Millie makes a quick retreat.

Em blows her nose with impressive force, and I wonder at what point in my life I will start carrying cloth tissues.

"Sorry," Em says softly.

"What for?" Millie and I say together.

"I...." Em says. "I just...I can't."

"Well," I say, once she finishes blowing her nose a second time, "you can decide to talk about it now." I am trying to keep from sounding too judgmental. "Or, you can decide not to talk about it again for, I don't know…about thirty more years."

Millie snort-laughs, a surprisingly youthful sound coming from such an old woman. "Longer than that."

"What?" That had been my plan, anyway. I'd been hoping to tell Joel and Sonya the truth about my mother's accident, and while that didn't happen this morning, hopefully, this doesn't mean that it never will.

"It's more like sixty years," Millie says.

"Seriously?" Em looks up to face her older selves. "You never talk about it?"

"I can't predict what will happen if I ever get out of here, but if you mean in my experience, in the sixty-year expanse between you and me?" Millie waggles her finger back and forth between her and Em. "You try once or twice, but nobody wants to hear it. Not your friends. Not your family. Not your father. Especially not your father. Other than Lord knows how many therapists you will pay to listen to you." She shakes her head. "The more I tried to talk about it with them, the more unstable they thought I was. Those alternative facts are firmly set in stone."

"They still say that?" I have to ask.

"Say what?" asks Em.

"Alternative facts," I say. "It's a Trump-era thing."

Millie shrugs. I guess that the political climate of the first quarter of the twenty-first century isn't something she thinks about a lot, it being, for her, now well into the middle quarter. Maybe the phrase *alternative facts* has just become part of the regular lexicon.

"Wait," says Em. "In all these years, you've never convinced *anyone* that I was, I mean we were, the ones who actually killed Mom?"

"We didn't *kill* her," Millie says softly. "It was an accident."

"Whatever. But it was my fault. Our fault." Em drops her gaze to the balled-up handkerchief in her hand. "You still believe that, right?"

Neither Millie nor I respond. Em knows full well that we

must believe it, at least on some level. Why else would we all be here?

"How can you live with that?" she asks.

Millie and I exchange a look, clueless as to what the proper answer entails. It's a question neither of us has ever been able to honestly answer.

Millie tries first. "I decided a long time ago that it is best to accept a truth I didn't fully believe to be true," she says. "You can shout it until you are blue in the face...and you have, Em. I know. But you have to accept that nobody is ever going to actually listen."

"Look," I say. "It had to be Dad at the wheel. I mean, for his sake, it had to be him. It's that parental impulse, you know? Like those stories you hear about mothers who pick up a car to save their kid stuck underneath? Except in Dad's case, it was all in his head, like a psychological rescue or something. Anyway, it doesn't matter who else believes us. It won't change anything." I drone on with this monologue, but I know I am bullshitting. I mean, why else was I so compelled to stir up this shit this morning if I didn't want to pull Sonya and Joel deeper into the story? My story. Our story. The decisions we made.

"I don't know," I say, mostly to myself, an acknowledgment of my failure. "I guess we'll all just have to make peace with the fact that we'll probably go to the grave being the only person who knows the full truth about what really happened."

"So you're saying you've both somehow made peace with the fact that Dad took the fall?" Em looks from one of us to the other.

"Not entirely," Millie says softly. "But I have accepted that it was an accident. It doesn't matter who was behind the wheel. The result would be the same."

"Of course it matters."

"Look," I say. "It's useless to belabor it. Nobody has ever believed us. It was too well documented."

"What do you mean?" Em asks.

"There were a lot of articles—"

"And books," Millie adds.

"And a television show," I say, biting my lip. It is a little embarrassing to think about.

Em looks to Millie, as if for confirmation. "Our father made a good living off the story rights," Millie says and shrugs apologetically.

"We all did," I add. "Even now it still pays the bills." I gesture toward one of the Bloomingdale's bags, now crumpled in the corner along with the rest of my belongings.

"There was a fierce bidding war for the memoir. Do you remember that, Emilia? He went up to New York for a few days. It was the first time he'd left me—us—alone in the house for so long. But when he came back, he drove up to the house in a new car?"

I nod. "Yeah. The red Beamer."

Em isn't having it. Her father wouldn't do that. He would never have indulged in anything so crass. "Bullshit," she says. "That's total bullshit."

"No, Em. It's not," I say. "Look." I tap on the phone and hold it up for the others to see. There is a folder full of documents and articles I've scanned over the years. Assuming the battery holds, these files might serve to refresh a few additional things.

POLICE REPORT

Case No. 1368
Reporting Officer: Jack Heron
Date: October 12, 1986
Time: 11:17 a.m.

INCIDENT

Detail of Event

On Monday, October 12, 1986, I, Officer Jack Heron, along with Officer Joseph Landry, was on uniformed patrol in marked cruiser E222. At approximately 11:17 a.m. we were dispatched to the southern end of the Bay Breeze Bridge. Dispatch had received a call from Kliber Farm. The caller, identified as Edith Shaw, 51, had been driving on the bridge and said she witnessed a red Audi sedan drive over the guardrail and plunge into the water. The caller immediately drove to the nearest location that might have a phone.

We arrived at the Bay Breeze Bridge at approximately 11:26, where we saw skid marks on the road, leading to the breached guardrail. Two people were in the water attempting to swim to the shoreline. Witnesses identified as John Patrick, 24, and Sarah Patrick, 23, described a red car plunge into the water, and then within a minute the two people surfaced, but they thought there might be another person in the car.

We immediately called for additional support, both for floatation devices to assist the swimmers and for an underwater rescue attempt. John Patrick offered to drive to the house located just off the northern end of the bridge, where he was able to retrieve two life rings from a boat docked at the private pier.

At 11:39, John Patrick threw the life rings to two people in the water, which they were able to swim to. A police boat driven by Officer Theodore Williams arrived a few minutes later, and they were able to get the people out of the water. The girl, identified as

Emilia Fletcher, had a large gash across her brow and was highly distraught, but was able to confirm that there had been another person in the car, her mother, Sally Fletcher, in the back seat. The father, Samuel Fletcher, appeared to be in shock and was, at first, unable to speak.

Officer Landry and I descended to the bank and, once the victims were calm enough, asked Mr. Fletcher to explain what had happened.

According to Mr. Fletcher, the car suddenly accelerated, and he was unable to maintain control and the car hit the rail. The car began to submerge, quickly gathering water through the open windows in the front of the car. Because the windows were open, Mr. Fletcher and his daughter were able to pull themselves out of the car. He says Mrs. Fletcher's seat belt appeared to be stuck and he wasn't able to help her out in time. He says that he and the girl tried to swim back down once they caught their breath, but they could not make it to the car as it had sunk too far.

The underwater rescue team arrived at approximately 12:15 p.m. Two divers, Felix Wiler and Frank Spatz, immediately dove into the bay. At approximately 12:20 p.m. they surfaced holding the body of a woman that Mr. Fletcher identified as his wife, Sally Fletcher. She was pronounced dead at the scene.

Samuel Fletcher and his daughter were taken in separate ambulances to St. Anthony's Hospital, as they were both exhibiting signs of hypothermia and the girl appeared to be concussed.

Actions Taken

Calls to bring up car so they can test to see whether there was a mechanical problem.

Summary

While there appears to be no foul play, it is necessary to recover the car for a full forensic analysis of the mechanical system.

The Washington Star
October 13, 1986

SALLY FLETCHER DIES IN CAR ACCIDENT

CO-ANCHOR OF WBS MORNING SHOW DROWNED IN SUBMERGED CAR, DAUGHTER AND HUSBAND SURVIVE

Bay Breeze, MD—Sally Fletcher, who in 1976 became the first woman to anchor WBS's *Sunrise America*, was pronounced dead early Sunday afternoon.

Police say Fletcher was in the back seat when the car she and her family were in spun out of control. The force of the impact broke the barrier on the Bay Breeze Bridge, and the car rapidly sank into the water. Her husband, novelist Samuel Fletcher, and their daughter, Emilia, were able to pull themselves out of the car windows. Both are in stable condition. Police say Mrs. Fletcher's seat belt was jammed and she was unable to pull herself free. Divers removed the body from the vehicle after 25 minutes.

Maryland State Police are investigating the accident.

Obituary Pages
The New York Herald
October 14, 1986

SALLY FLETCHER, A TELEVISION STAR JOURNALIST WHO BROKE BARRIERS AND CHARMED PRESIDENTS, IS DEAD AT 48.

Sally Fletcher, whose elegant demeanor and erudite wit charmed millions of Americans each morning from her anchor seat at WBS's *Sunrise America* for the last 11 years, died on Sunday in a car accident near her vacation home in Bay Breeze, Maryland.

With her determined spirit, the former catalog model began her television career at WBS-TV in Atlanta, Georgia, where she hosted an early morning program called *Sally at Sunrise*. The show featured local celebrities and politicians and won a regional Emmy after just one year on the air. It did not take long for the networks to take notice of Fletcher's subtle humor and ability to gracefully disarm even the most polished of politicians before they were aware of what was at play.

"She was a rare breed of woman," said Sanders Forest, the WBS President who first hired Fletcher as a general correspondent out of the news network's Washington, DC, bureau. "Her ability to charm and disarm everyone from first-term congressmen to heads of state never failed to amaze me."

Fletcher was named senior anchor of *Sunrise America* in 1976, the first woman ever to anchor a program at the network since its inception in 1954. Sally Fletcher is survived by her husband, novelist Samuel Fletcher, and their daughter, Emilia.

Herald Times Book World
Review: *Today Is a Brand New Day: A Memoir of Love, Loss, and Redemption* by Samuel K. Fletcher
By Tracey Lowe-Blaine.

On October 13, 1986, there was a shrouded chair in the television studio when the nation's preeminent morning news program broadcast went on air. Gone was the luminescent and beloved host, Sally Fletcher, who had drowned in a horrific car accident one day before. Her death was a shock for the millions of fans she referred to as her morning family. For her actual family, whose adventures and joys she so often shared with the rest of the world in the course of her broadcast, her death was catastrophic. For her husband, the novelist Samuel Fletcher, it was even worse. Fletcher was driving the car at the time of the accident, and in *New Day* he writes about his public reckoning with guilt and the subsequent redemption he finds by allowing himself and his daughter to embrace the memories of the short time they had together.

In lyrical although sometimes cloying prose, Fletcher pays great homage to the memory of his wife, tracing their story from their first date to her rapid ascent through the glass ceiling of the news networks. The title itself is a nod to the catchphrase Sally Fletcher turned into household vernacular. With dramatic plotting, he creates not just a compelling narrative, but a near playbook for other ambitious young women to follow.

This is not Mr. Fletcher's first foray into storytelling. His first book, *The Flying Trapeze*, a well-received mystery novel about the murder of a circus performer, was published more than ten years ago. In *New Day*, while grappling with his deep sense of guilt and shame, he clearly breaks out of the writer's block that had plagued him for so long. What emerges is a confident and sympathetic storyteller with a fascinating insight into the personal life of a famous person.

REVIEW OF TELEVISION SERIES
The New York Star

Review: *In Memory's Wake*, a new series premiering on ABC on Friday, Matthew McConaughey stars as the bereaved father who accidentally caused the dramatic death of his famous wife. Based loosely on Samuel Fletcher's memoir, *Today Is a Brand New Day*, the show alters between titillating looks at the glamorous life of the '80s superstar anchor Sally Fletcher and the shadow cast by her untimely death.

12

Study Hall: Emilia

October 12
3:43 p.m.
Friendship Heights Metro
Washington, DC

The elevator lights have gone out again, but the otherwise impenetrable darkness is penetrated by the glow of my phone. We are gathered in the center of the floor, crowded around the device as if it were a tiny campfire, Millie and I watching as Em swipes back and forth from one document to the next.

It takes her only a few minutes to figure out how to turn the pages on the phone, how to operate a universe in the palm of her hand. For her, after all, it is 1987, and the closest she has come to seeing a smartphone was while watching episodes of *Inspector Gadget* on Saturday mornings in third grade. Or maybe it was *Get Smart*. I loved those shows. Either way, she can't quite seem to get over the fact that the entirety of her life—her past and her future—is held in this strange rectangular device, but she's getting the hang of it. It isn't all that surprising, I guess. Pretty much everyone under the age of eighteen seems to have a sixth sense for figuring these things out. It is amazing to watch, though, how quickly Em does it, first holding the phone out like a talisman, then bringing it close to her face as if she is going to sniff it. She taps on the screen and seems then to instinctively get it, as if she has been using it her entire life. It reminds me of Sonya at five when she got hold of my phone. I didn't even know that she had been playing with it or even knew how to use it until a few days later when I found the selfie video she had taken, intently wiggling her eyebrows and then saying sweetly into the camera, "I'm gonna, um, wiggle my eyebrows now," and then doing just that and adding, "Isn't that cool?"

That was a lifetime ago. These days I am fully aware that Sonya is using a smartphone, all right. All of the time. Joel and I fight about that too. Joel had wanted to wait until she was in eighth grade to get her one, but I was anxious about that walk home from the bus after school. It was all of five blocks, but things happen, right?

They do.

Of course, as Joel seems pleased to regularly point out, the thing that happened wasn't that Sonya got abducted or mugged, but rather that she got lost in the void of the ether, nose to screen for way too many of her waking hours, and instead of the device giving me a way to connect with her, it has pulled us further apart.

That's not what is happening here.

Here, Em is narrowing in on a review of the television series based on my—her—father's book. The article features a photograph of the two of us at the premiere. Em easily figures out how to enlarge it, how to zoom in on the image by stretching her thumb and forefinger across the screen. There I am—just a few years older than she is now—wearing the long black sleeveless dress my mother had bought for me to accompany her to one of the many events she attended, but which I had tossed into a heap in the back of my closet instead, only pulling it out and ironing it a few years after she died.

Em swipes to the next one, another article from the day after the crash. The documents are not well organized, but there are a lot of them. If my brief career in journalism had taught me anything, it taught me how to locate old clips.

"Where did you get all of this?" Em asks.

I look at Millie. "Well?" I say, because Millie should know how I got all of these documents. She was there, after all.

Except Millie says she doesn't remember. Not really. "Don't look at me," she says. "It's been a long while since I've touched a device like that."

I suppress the urge to find out what—if my future self no longer has such a device—do people in the future use to communicate. "*I* didn't get all of this. You did. When you, we, whatever, after college."

"Which college?" Em is intrigued by this sliver of information. Much of her focus this fall has been on completing college applications, after all. It's been drilled into her since before she could speak that college will be the single biggest determinant in shaping the trajectory of her life. That's not completely wrong. But it's not completely right either.

"Tufts," Millie says, and Em looks upset. Brown is her first choice.

"Don't worry, dear," says Millie. "It turns out okay."

Or maybe it doesn't, I want to say, because Tufts was where I met Joel, and right now, Sonya aside, sometimes I wish I hadn't. But it was there that I started to pull all of these documents together, that I finally had enough distance from the accident to start investigating it more clinically.

"I spent a lot of time in the library culling through microfiche and making copies," I explain. "There was a folder about six inches thick. I still haven't had the chance to scan it all."

"And that doesn't account for the stacks of videotapes," Millie adds. "The story was everywhere."

"I have some of those too," I say. "I just had some of them digitized. But you would need internet access to stream them from my drive."

"You need what?" asks Em, who has yet to experience even a fax.

"It doesn't matter. And anyway, it's too hard to explain," I say. "Just know that the world will start to look very different very quickly."

"You have no idea," says Millie, to me more than to Em.

"Regardless," I say, shaking her off. "The mediums change, but the story doesn't."

"What's that supposed to mean?" Em asks brusquely. Her sudden shift in tone startles me, but when she follows up with a head-shaking, exasperated spit of "Jesus Christ!" I have to laugh.

Because of course.

Em is me, and here she is behaving not unlike my own pubescent daughter, who has hormones coursing through her veins and blurring her sanity. Sonya is younger than I was when I first got my period, that's true. Probably something in the milk. The formula I gave in to when breastfeeding failed. The fucking air we breathe. Who knows? But lately it feels like if I so much as poke the kid, she might explode. These days, her normally sweet demeanor is routinely tainted by a snotty new tone. It's like a siren call warning of the impending torrent of hormonal shifts.

I look at Em, who is back with her nose to the screen, jaw dropped in amazement at whatever image or article she is absorbing. She's so Jekyll and Hyde-like it's ridiculous.

Millie and I grin at each other. We are thinking the same thing. We don't have to say it; I can see it on her face. I just can't believe how much I let it get under my skin when Sonya acts like that. Sweet one second, spewing venom the next.

What's so insane, now that I think of it, is that everything that has happened—almost everything about the horrific event that has shaped my life, our lives—is fundamentally linked to an unstable phenomenon that has hounded human lives for millennia, not just mine. I am positive Millie is thinking the same thing. I can see it in her eyes. This is at the heart of the matter. Well, maybe not the heart. It's really about a different organ all three of us have shared. Which is our brain. More specifically, it's the brain as it exists inside Em's skull at this moment. This is what I am thinking about, and I am pretty sure Millie is too. We are watching Em as she pokes around on the phone, mesmerized, and we are thinking about how easy it is, with such a specimen in our rearview mirrors, to choose to forget that just like our daughter—and just like Em right now—we, too, were once driven by those bizarre synaptic fits, those impulsive moments of idiocy that can only be attributed to an immature prefrontal cortex, those hormonal fits of rage that, to the uninitiated, appear to be completely irrational, but to the teenager hosting the three-pound mass of muscle inside of her head make absolutely complete sense.

Really, we are thinking—I am practically composing an essay about it, imagining what I want to say the next time Joel and I start to tangle about Sonya—it is a tad insane that we even allow such mercurial beings, such lax guardians of such a delicate matter, to do things like turn on a gas stove, babysit a toddler, or worse, take control of the two-ton mass that is the modern automobile and let them drive it faster than the fastest land animal on earth.

This is the irreconcilable truth about the shape of my life, the shape of everyone's life: the actions we take and the choices we make when our brains are still being baked have the potential to completely change the trajectory of our lives in irreparable ways. We all unwittingly make decisions when we are young that will change the course of our lives. They aren't always big decisions, like where to go to college or whom to marry. They can be small and seemingly insignificant. And not unlike that butterfly in the Galapagos whose flapping of wings causes a tsunami in California (okay, I have to admit that's probably slightly overstated, although conceptually it works), Em's small decision (my small decision) about whether to have pancakes or toast one fall morning when she was sixteen set off a series of events that would change the course of her (our) life (lives), ultimately leading to her (our, my, whatever) worst decision of all.

But that final fateful decision needs some context. It needs to start with the first domino of bad decisions that led up to it, a decision we made on Saturday night, Columbus Day Weekend—back when they still called it that—October 11, 1986.

13

THE DAY BEFORE: EM

October 11, 1986
7:23 p.m.
Brandywine Street, NW
Washington, DC

Em didn't want to join her parents in Bay Breeze. She didn't want to be with her parents anywhere, for that matter. She wanted to be at a house party in Chevy Chase that some of her friends were planning to attend. She was intrigued by this, never having attended one of these notorious parentless bashes before. She had heard about these parties (she was nearly done with high school, after all). She had heard about the kegs that piled up in the backyards, about kids making out in every crevice of the house, about other kids vomiting over hedges. It wasn't her scene. What kid, truly, in their heart of hearts, wants to be thrown into a chaotic and confusing situation like that? Okay, most kids. At least they think they want to be thrown into such a situation because their friends say they want to, and we all know how that goes.

Which is how it went for Em. In her heart of hearts, she didn't really want to go, but she went. She lined her eyes with the metallic turquoise liner her mom had given her, a sample that was sent to the show, then she wiped it off and went with her familiar black instead. She pulled on a pair of faded jeans and tucked them into bunched-up pink socks and then laced up her white Tretorn sneakers. A simple green sweater from Benetton finished the look. It was an outfit she wouldn't be caught dead in now, just one year later.

Her friend Amy waited for her at the Tenleytown Metro station, about five blocks from her house. They took the train one stop to Friendship Heights, ascended in our now-familiar elevator, stepped onto the rust-colored tiles leading out from the street-level platform to Wisconsin Avenue, and then walked the full mile into the suburban tree-lined streets of Chevy Chase as the sun was starting to set and the fall chill made Em regret her decision not to wear a coat.

As they approached the house where the party was being hosted, she felt an even deeper chill. Call it a premonition, but the house was imposing—a haughty faux-Tudor manse, complete with crosshatched frames over heavy lead-glass windows and high-pitched roofs with decorative half-timbering. To Em, the medieval design had a very specific and sinister tone, as one might imagine a haunted house in a children's book, a monster's mansion high on a hill, an evil lair manicured to mask its actual mission. She mentioned this to Amy, who told her to relax, told her that she was just trying to talk herself out of having a good time. It felt like a dare. Em charged up the walkway, pulling Amy behind her, decidedly determined to do just that.

The memories are snapshots. A crush of bodies here. The damp condensation of the keg on the porch over there. Billy Idol crooning in the background. She remembers the beer splashing out of the large plastic cup that was shoved into her hand. But long story short, she remembers very little of what happened next, except for the moment, probably a couple of hours later, when Christopher Grant—big, handsome, Ivy-destined, lacrosse-playing Christopher Grant—somehow, she doesn't remember how, had her head in his oversized hands and was pushing her down toward his crotch when she suddenly became that vomiting kid, and she threw up not on a hedge or in a toilet, but all over the brown corduroy pants of the most popular boy in school.

One humiliation compounded by another humiliation. A pyramid of humiliations built on an ill-informed decision about how to have a good time.

The next thing she remembers is someone, probably Amy, pushing her headfirst into a taxi, barking instructions, throwing cash at the driver, and slamming the door. She remembers being packed into the back seat of her family car in the dark of night, hurtling toward their country house in Maryland's Eastern Shore, feeling like someone was trying to bore through her head with a power drill and uncertain if she could make it the whole drive without vomiting again.

And then she remembers lying in her room in their country house. The only light came from the hallway and her mother was in silhouette when she pulled off Em's socks and tucked the blanket around her shoulders.

"That was really stupid, Em," she said, and then, in a rare moment of tenderness, she gently kissed her daughter on the forehead. The saccharine cloud of her mother's perfume only made Em feel worse.

"You'll be fine, Emilia. I promise. Tomorrow we'll get you cleaned up. Believe me, I've had enough experience to know a good hangover cure or two."

Then the hallway light was switched off, Em fell asleep, and this in turn brings her to breakfast, to her mother's answer to her daughter's hangover in the form of a question. Pancakes or toast?

14

PANCAKES OR TOAST: EM

October 12, 1986
9:23 a.m.
Bay Breeze, MD

As with most things that happen unexpectedly, initially there was nothing special about that particular morning, nothing to otherwise plant a marker in Emilia's memory. This fact is compounded by the fuzz from her hangover, and because of this her memory of the first part of that particular morning has remained a composite memory of so many mornings in their country home, of waking up to the white rays of light filtering through the drawn curtains, of the scent of her dad's coffee percolating in the kitchen.

The likely scenario is that on that morning, Emilia—Em at the time—would have stayed in her bed for a few minutes before the pressure from her bladder won out—an unfortunate trait that, as already established, will remain consistent throughout her life. She would then have padded her way into the sun-filled kitchen where her father would be staring out the window, past their turquoise-blue kidney-shaped pool, watching the boats and the birds moving across the horizon.

"Hey, pumpkin. How'd you sleep?" her father would have asked as he finished stirring milk and sugar into a cup of coffee, a process that would have started the moment he heard her descending the stairs and finished as Em walked into the kitchen when he handed it to her.

That morning he might have also handed her some aspirin, because it was his nature to do things like guide her through her first hangover. "World's Best Dad?" she would have asked, turning the mug in her hands as she read the large printed words embossed on the ceramic.

"Just thought I would remind you," he'd say, and they would laugh at the joke that was part of the pattern.

Em did love her father. That was never in question. And he, of course, loved her, even though it was because of her that he had told his publisher he was going to miss yet another deadline. "Just one school year left, Emmie. Then you spring from the nest," he had told her when they were laying out their summer plans the previous spring. "The novel can wait." Em nodded, but she knew there was more to his seemingly intractable writer's block than his fatherly devotion. It had been years since he published his last book.

So she played along, and on that morning they would have likely sat together at the kitchen counter, sipping sweet, milky coffee in front of the picture window, watching the activity on the bay start to build. It spread out before them, as wide as an ocean. The fishing boats, out since dawn, were now returning to one of the docks scattered along the coast. Sometimes a small sailboat would drift past, or a larger catamaran. If it was a motorized vehicle passing, it might elicit a curse. "Fucking polluters," her father would say, and she would chastise him like she used to do when she was little, demanding a punitive dime, for old times' sake. To which he would say, "Fuck that," because it can be funny when adults say shockingly inappropriate things.

Maybe he said that. Maybe not. It was the sort of joke he might make, but it's hard to know. It wasn't one of the details the detectives wrote down.

Neither was the fact that the phone first rang at approximately 9:35 a.m.

That is the start of when Emilia's memories become more distinct. The loud, abrasive sound ripped the coarse fabric of her hangover, waking her up more than any amount of coffee could have done. Nobody ever called them on Sunday mornings, not this early, and definitely not her mom, since in normal circumstances, at that hour on a weekend morning she would have been sleeping upstairs.

So in her memory, the bulky tan phone hanging from the wall had a horrifically loud ring. Her father answered and mouthed to Em that it was her mother calling.

"Why are you at Jake's?" he asked. Jake's General Store—one of those quaint country stores that never changes, complete with jars of candy that can be bought with a few coins and a bulletin board covered with notices for local services and tag sales—was down at the end of the road. This was out of character. Not only was her mother not asleep upstairs, she never did the shopping.

Her father covered the mouthpiece and told Em that her mother wanted to know if Em would like pancakes for breakfast or if she preferred that her mother bring home some jam and a freshly baked loaf of bread sold at the front of the store. It would be nice with the farm fresh eggs they sell, he added.

The three women in the elevator remember this clearly because everyone remembers things when they are different, when they deviate from the norm.

"She's at the store?" Em asked. "Why is she at the store?"

Her father had a little smirk along with his shrug, so she figured her parents were in cahoots about something, although she wasn't sure what. "Pancakes or toast?" he repeated.

Em chose pancakes.

One minute later, her mother called again. Jake's was out of maple syrup. She suggested they come get her and they all drive into town for brunch instead.

Which is what they decided to do.

They had breakfast at the Bay Breeze Inn. They sat at their usual corner table with the checkerboard tablecloth and view of the water, and her mother ordered a Bloody Mary. "Hair of the dog," she said with a wink and offered a small sip to her daughter. She then proceeded, instead of a meal, to drink down two more.

After that, after a brunch that consisted of pancakes with greasy eggs and burnt bacon on the side, it requires another turn to primary source materials to piece together what happened next. That is, to further lay out the consequence of deciding to have pancakes rather than toast.

15

Drinking Games: Emilia

October 12
4:27 p.m.
Friendship Heights Metro
Washington, DC

"I've never thought about that," says Em, touching the pathologist's note on the autopsy report I pulled up on my phone. *Blood alcohol concentration .096%. Impaired.*

The light has been holding steady for half an hour or so, and Em's chipped neon-green nail polish is glimmering in the cold fluorescent light as she taps the screen. Neon green was definitely an '80s-era shade. Funny how just this morning, three decades on, Sonya was sporting the same color on her nails. I almost say something about history repeating itself but decide to stay on the topic at hand.

"You haven't thought about the fact that Mom may have had one too many Bloody Marys that morning?" I ask my younger self, not remembering when it was that she—I—first might have entertained that very same thought.

"I just assumed Mom was stuck in the car because her seat belt buckle was jammed," says Em. "That's why Dad couldn't get her out. He couldn't hold his breath long enough to help both me and her."

"The mechanical reports were inconclusive about the latch being jammed," I say.

"What about these?" asks Em, zooming in on—she's already figured out how to do that—an image in the report. It is an outline of a human form, front and back. An X is marked on the forehead, and there is one just at the edge of each hand, each showing areas of injury. Em is pointing at those.

"What about them? She was probably just fumbling to get out but too drunk and disoriented to do it," I say, sinking back into my respective base, propped up with the flotsam of cast-off jackets and folded-up shirts that now make up what is essentially my nest.

Just as my butt touches the floor, Em bolts up.

"Fuck!" she blurts out. Clearly, she has placed the new piece of information into her puzzle of that day. "Fuck, fuck, fuck!"

"What is it?" asks Millie.

"So that's our fault too?" Em demands, adding another "fuck!" for good measure.

"What do you mean, dear?"

"I mean, she was drunk. She ordered the drinks because of me. And don't 'dear' me."

"You didn't make her order them, Em," Millie says.

"Yeah, right. Of course I did."

"You didn't get her drunk," I pipe in. "That's ridiculous."

"Is it?" Em turns to me. "You probably have kids around my age, right?"

"Well…not exactly—"

"But are you a mother? Do you have kids?"

"One. A daughter, actually," I say this slowly, because it must be strange for this seventeen-year-old girl in front of me to learn that she has a child less than a decade younger than she is right now. "She's in sixth grade."

Em digests this. She looks at Millie, who has moved back to her corner of the elevator. "So I guess you're a mom too, right? I mean, obviously. But now she's, whatever, I can't do the math." She calculates it in her head anyway. "She's forty-two? Who knows, maybe you're even a grandmother by now?"

Millie nods in the affirmative, which makes me skip a breath.

"Okay, fine," Em says, getting to her point. "So if your daughter, or granddaughter or whatever, threw a tantrum in a public place and almost got you kicked out of the restaurant, wouldn't that drive you to drink?"

"I don't remember doing that," I say.

"You don't? You don't remember how we sat there at the restaurant and as soon as I, we, you know what I mean…as soon as I started to tell Mom and Dad about the party and how much alcohol there was, about the kegs and the plastic cups scattered across the front yard…Mom just launched in about how it was so ironic because the drinking age just got changed, and Christopher's dad was one of the politicians behind the push to make that happen. Don't you remember that?"

That particular fact is one that anyone who was a high school student in the DC area in the late 1980s would remember. In 1986, the District was one of the last places in the country where the drinking age was still eighteen; conservative politicians made it the cause du jour and were threatening to pull funding for the city unless that changed. There were photos of Congressman Clifford Grant parading around with DC Mayor Marion Barry, pushing for a higher drinking age in the District even though he represented Maryland. It had been bubbling for a while, but a horrific accident that September that caused the death of two inebriated teenagers had clinched the deal. Christopher Grant's dad was all over the cause, and he was all over the news. Clifford Grant, the great conservative crusader, saving area teens from cirrhosis. Or whatever. Christopher was teased relentlessly about it, but as an eighteen-year-old he benefited from the grandfather clause and was still able to buy booze as he saw fit—and anyway, all the public squabbling had granted kids with means plenty of time to work up scores of fake IDs.

Back at the Bay Breeze Inn, my mother was eating it up. She was all "Christopher Grant's house? Christopher, the son of Congressman Clifford Grant?" and then she just wanted to talk about that, not about what happened to me on that particular night.

16

COMING OF AGE: EM

October 12, 1986
10:33 a.m.
Bay Breeze, MD

"Yes, Mother. *That* Christopher," Em muttered, pushing the remains of her syrup-saturated pancake around with her fork.

"Oh, that's too good." Her mother laughed gleefully. "He seems like such a nice kid, though. Is he?"

No. Not really. But Em wasn't sure how to articulate that fact. Not that she was so sure he wasn't a nice kid, that she wasn't somehow complicit in what had happened, that it might somehow have been partially her fault. But she was sure that whoever was to blame, the bottom line was that she had humiliated herself in front of the coolest kids at her school.

She wanted to cry. Instead, she just shrugged and kept her gaze riveted on the glass saltshaker next to her plate.

"Oh, come on, Em," her mother whispered, as if they were conspiring. "He's so cute too." She reached over to pat Em's hand, but Em slipped her own away. "Well, then…" She turned to Em's father with a wink. Em looked out the window and stared at the horizon. "I guess I'm onto something, aren't I?" her mother said. "Wouldn't they be a sweet couple, Sam? Don't you think?"

He turned to Em instead. "You okay there, kiddo?"

Em was not okay. Her eyes were hot and red and desperate for a few moistening tears that refused to materialize.

"I'm fine," she said.

"Oh, Em," her mother said with an exaggerated sigh. "Don't be that way. I was just teasing."

"Yeah, right," Em said under breath. "More like you were praying."

"What's that?"

"You heard me." Em turned around to stare directly into her mother's eyes. Her mother, perfectly coiffed even on a lazy weekend morning, with her silky blond hair tied into an effortless-looking French twist and her subtle eyeshadow glimmering just so. As a teenager, her mother probably had boys tripping over themselves to be near her, but then, Em was equally sure, they would find themselves cowering in her icy presence.

"That's what you want, right?" Em demanded. "You want a daughter who dates the son of a congressman, like that would somehow make me less embarrassing to you than I already am?"

"Oh, honey, I—"

"No, it's true. There's nothing about me that helps you anymore, right? The fabulous Sally Fletcher can't trot me out on TV like you used to, when you could get me all frilled up for your dog-and-pony show. Now—" Em tugged on the worn-out gray sweatshirt she was wearing. With its torn collar, the sweatshirt's neckline fell off one shoulder, revealing the strap of the faded black tank top she'd worn underneath. "Not exactly your little designer baby, am I?"

"Em, you're being ridiculous." She pointed a manicured coral-polished finger at Em's chest. "I am sure that torn sweatshirts are all the rage these days. That *Flashdance* style? You look adorable. And you're my daughter. Of course I'm proud of you. Right, Sam?" She turned to her husband for support. "Of course I'm proud of her."

"Of course your mother is proud of you," he parroted. "I am too."

"For what?" Em said, her voice rising. "For getting sick drunk at Clifford Grant's house? For getting Bs?"

"You mostly get As, Em," her father corrected.

"So, for not being a total loser?" Em snapped back.

"For being you," her mother said softly, a vague assertion that did not encourage confidence in an insecure sixteen-year-old. And Em, exhausted, her head still throbbing, her pre-frontal cortex awash in a soup of adolescent hormones, her anger-stoking amygdala practically on fire, well, she just kind of lost it.

The specific details of this tantrum are impossible to recall because it was largely just a torrent of venom spat this way and that, but mostly at herself.

Her parents begged her to calm down. There were people looking at them. This was embarrassing. But Em went on. She was spewing word salad, and it only ended with the waiter coming by to ask her to please lower her voice as other customers were getting upset.

That small distraction, that little interruption of the flow, was sufficient to break Em's frenzy and return her to a more ra-tional state, one in which she was simply crying and apologizing for her behavior, blowing her nose and saying, almost as a non sequitur, that she wished her parents trusted her a little more, that she wasn't a baby and she could fend for herself.

"Of course we trust you." Her father reached for her hand and she didn't whip it away. "Tell you what. You need to clock some miles on that learner's permit of yours. How about you drive us home? Would you like that? A little adrenaline rush to get your sea legs back on?"

"The new car?" her mother asked. She held her glass up, gesturing toward the window. "It's still raining, Sam."

"It's just a drizzle. What difference does it make? Em, what do you say?"

Em thought about it. Her head still hurt and she was ex-hausted by her outcry, but maybe it would help. She could take her mind off Christopher Grant, bond with her parents over this rite of passage, get a few more miles under her belt. She decided that yes, she would like to drive them home.

"I'll surely need another drink if we are going to do that," her mother said, not unkindly. They each let out a small anxi-ety-flavored laugh, and Sally Fletcher waved a finger in the air, calling to the waiter, "I'll have another one, please."

17

SKINCARE ROUTINES: EMILIA

October 12
5:32 p.m.
Friendship Heights Metro
Washington, DC

The spells of interaction are periodically broken by stretches of awkward silence induced by the sporadic changes in light.

When the light flickers on, sometimes the three of us talk, cautiously inquiring about our future and our past, not fully sure how many details we are each ready to know, or share, or remember. Sometimes we just stare at each other, which can create either a bittersweet sort of pleasure or a heart-tightening sort of dread, depending on who I am looking at or what memory it jogs.

When the light flickers off, the darkness in the elevator becomes library-quiet and the sounds of our breathing and movements are amplified, making the thoughts flying around in my head feel like shrieks and making my non-visual senses more keenly attuned.

In the dark, I hear what sounds like the wrinkling of a candy wrapper coming from Millie's side of the space.

"Did you find something else to eat?" I ask.

"Unfortunately, no," she says. "It's just a pack of tissues."

"You have tissues? Are you serious? We could have used them, you know, instead of my new shirts?"

"I forgot they were in here."

"You forgot? How many hours have we had to sit around rummaging through our bags? I think I know the contents of mine by heart."

"All of the bags?" Millie asks.

"Yes," I say. "All of them."

This is mostly true. The contents of my shopping bags—the aforementioned shirts, a jacket, a new pair of pants—have, by this time, all been utilized either as cushioning or as cleaning supplies. My red suede handbag, that's another story. I stick my hand in to check, fishing around slowly lest Millie hear me, hear this concession that her implication might be right.

And yes, I can feel what I think is an old, plastic-shrouded Kind bar. I leave that alone. But deep in the lint-filled crevices along the interior seams at the very bottom, folded under one of the seams, I find something else.

"I stand corrected. There's a nail file." I run a finger over the flat metal stick pressing into my palm. "Maybe it could be useful somehow?"

"To file us out of here?" Millie asks dismissively.

"Don't be so negative," I say, which elicits a snort from Em's corner. "I thought you were asleep over there, Em."

"I wish," she mutters. "At least that would help pass the time."

"So you're just sitting there stewing?"

"Aren't we all?"

"Actually, no. I am sitting here trying to calmly and lucidly think about how we can move on from this."

"What else do you think I'd be stewing about?"

"Well, we can't just sit here sulking and bickering and waiting for the inevitable."

"And what would that be?" asks Millie. "The inevitable?"

Death would be an obvious answer. Maybe rescue, although given the complication of this apparent time warp, that is becoming hard to conceive. Nobody responds, and we sink back into a consuming silence until suddenly the light snaps back on, replacing the vertiginous darkness with a blinding white light that briefly causes strange circles and spots in my vision.

"Jesus," Em says, squinting. She looks around. I am exactly where she saw me last, sunk deep into my belongings.

I can feel her staring, and I start to feel a bit self-conscious, which is absurd, considering we are the same person and she has already seen plenty of me. But I guess that is part of my problem—the fact that I have never quite been able to settle into my own skin.

I look at Millie, in the opposite corner. She is fully reclined, lying on her back with her body stretched out across the length of her wall, her head propped up by her purse and her hands clasped on top of her stomach. She looks like she's either lounging on a tanning bed or resting in a coffin. Her eyes are closed against the glare of the light, allowing me to do what Em is doing—taking me in and trying to process what we will someday become.

Millie's white hair is thick and cut into the shapely bob that is now framing her face. She wears it well. For a moment I feel a small touch of pride in the fact that my older self is so nicely put together, that she didn't just throw in the towel and let herself fall apart. Except there are all of those age spots and a weirdly smooth forehead. Her skin is vaguely waxy and mask-like. It doesn't look right.

I can feel Em's focus shifting from me to Millie, where her gaze lands for some time. It's easier to stare at someone whose eyelids are closed.

"What are you thinking?" I ask, curious. That's a hard leap to make, seventeen to forty-seven, and on to the next.

"What?" Em says guiltily. "Nothing,"

"Oh, come on. You're seventeen, and you are literally staring into the face of your future self. You can't be thinking nothing."

"Fine," Em says. "It's just weird, you know? Like, am I really going to look like…?" It would be rude to complete that thought out loud, but I get where she's going.

"It's not a given."

"What do you mean?"

"Use more sunblock and you won't have to do that."

I point to my forehead and pantomime pressing a syringe.

"What is that supposed to mean?"

"Never mind. It's just…look, if it makes you feel any better, if you have ever read anything about time travel, and I know that you have, what happens once we leave this place will probably change what happens to that," I say, wagging a finger at Millie's face.

"Got it," Em says. "More sunblock. Seems really relevant right now."

"Now, that's not much of a compliment, now is it?" Millie says. Her eyes are still closed, but her tone is good-natured. She isn't offended.

"Oh," I say. "I guess you're not sleeping either?"

"Unfortunately, no." Stiffly, Millie attempts to rise to a sitting position. I reach out a hand to help pull her up.

"Thank you, dear." Millie gazes up at my face, which I know is starting to show some wear. I am sure she notices the wrinkles around my eyes, the crepey skin at my neck. Time has hardly left me alone. "You shouldn't be so judgmental, Emilia," Millie says, after taking a moment to smooth down her hair and straighten out her blouse. "It's unbecoming."

"I'm not saying you look bad," I say. "But I might argue that freezing one's face in the hopes of looking like you did a few decades before is also unbecoming."

"You do realize you have just inadvertently given yourself a compliment?"

"What?"

"You just said I don't look bad."

"You don't. I mean, for someone your age," I say, averting my gaze. I have never been good at accepting compliments, much less giving one to myself, which is essentially what is happening here.

"And neither do you. But don't tell me you haven't considered having some work done."

This is true. I don't like looking in the mirror anymore. Every day some new insult appears, but I like to think of myself as a feminist, and injections and plastic surgery feel antithetical to that. I also know that I look better now than I ever will again. And, of course, Em looks better than I have in years, bad eyeliner and half-grown-out bangs aside. "Botox just seems so extreme," I say. "And sort of self-hating."

Millie sighs. "We do have some talent in that arena, don't we?"

"It wasn't a hard talent to develop." I jut out my chin in Em's direction. "Living a lie can do that to a person."

"I think you mean living with a truth," says Em.

"Yes," Millie agrees. "One that no one else believes."

"So is that what this is about? May as well just live a lie?" I say.

"What is that supposed to mean?"

"Your Botox injections. That's not unlike lying, if you think about it."

"What is Botox?" Em asks.

"That's what I was showing you," I say, repeating the syringe pantomime. "It's a treatment for wrinkles. They inject small amounts of botulism in your face and it freezes the muscles so the wrinkles smooth out. Like this." I grab my cheeks and pull the skin taut. "You have to repeat it every few months," I mutter through stretched-out lips.

"Botulism?" says Em. "Are you kidding me? Doesn't that kill you?"

I let go and my face falls back into place. There's elasticity there yet. "Not necessarily."

"It's a different chemical now," Millie says. "Completely safe."

"It sounds barbaric," says Em.

"Blame the patriarchy?" I say, one eyebrow raised.

"Still the comedienne," says Millie.

"Again," Em says, "she's not that funny. But I still don't get it."

I get it. More than I am willing to admit to Millie.

Millie catches me staring at her.

"It's like looking into a distorted mirror, isn't it?" she asks.

I laugh and wink with my left eye. Millie winks with her right, mirroring me. I do it with my right eyelid, and she winks with her left. We both stick out our tongues.

"Take a closer look if you want," Millie says. She cups her hands under her chin, her manicured knobby fingers creating a decorative frame. "Tell me. What do you really think?" She slowly turns her head one way, then the other.

"What do I think? Honestly?"

"Is there any other way?"

"Fair enough. I think you look good, just a little mismatched. Your face doesn't look—how old are you again? Seventy-seven? Your brow and cheeks are smoother than your hands and neck. And it's strange how much thinner your eyelashes are. And your eyebrows too—they don't move. I've always had a soft spot for our eyebrows, you know? They have personality. Yours look like they've had their life sucked out of them."

"Em?" Millie turns to the girl, eyelashes fluttering since she can't wiggle her brows. "What's your take on this situation?"

Em leans in to get a better look at Millie's face. She is so close they can probably smell the staleness of each other's breath.

"A little space, dear," Millie says. "This close and you turn blurry."

Em pulls back. She studies Millie's regal jawline and her white hair, then turns to me, as if she is comparing my still full and mobile brows to Millie's. Her eyes dart from one older self to the other, and a single tear slowly rolls down her cheek.

"What? What do you see?" Millie asks.

Em sniffles and wipes her eyes with the back of her wrist. "I..." she starts to say, but she can't get the words out.

"I know," I say, placing a hand on Em's knee as if to say, *I'll take it from here.* "When I look at you, I think I see her too."

Em nods; she knows where I am going. She sees a flash of something in those tweezed-out brows, that near-platinum shade of hair.

"Mom," I say. "She sees Mom."

18

MID-CENTURY MODERN: MILLIE

October 12, 2047
7:30 a.m.
Brandywine Street, NW
Washington, DC

The toast was once again a little too burnt around the edges. There was a simple fix, of course; she could just turn the knob to a lower setting, but Millie felt more inclined to have something to rail against than not, and usually having nobody else in her home to argue with, this daily confrontation with the toaster had become energizing for her, like a strong cup of coffee.

She pinched the crust with her fingertips and threw the bread onto a china plate rimmed with a blue and gold floral pattern.

Millie had recently decided to start using those ornate antique dishes. She had inherited the Wedgewood set from her father decades before, along with the house, and it had remained untouched in the cabinet where her mother had left it decades before that. It had stayed untouched until Sally—Millie's ten-year-old granddaughter, named for Millie's mother, the late great Sally Fletcher—had been dispatched to help her pack up for the move to the assisted living apartment that Sonya had recently leased for her, even though Millie herself was stubbornly refusing to move out.

It was her house, after all. So what if it was too big for one person? So what if her daughter thought she was too frail to live on her own? So what if her daughter wanted more space? Sonya, who was acting like the caring daughter she wasn't now that there was something she wanted. Sonya, who after years of holding her own daughter back from her grandmother had finally let the girl off the leash when so little time remained.

No.

Millie wasn't having it. She was the last holdout on the street, having outlived her mother and her father and having finally found some semblance of peace in her ancestral home. She wasn't going anywhere.

A couple of weeks earlier, when she was having her semi-burnt toast on a less formal white plate, Millie sensed someone coming up the front steps. After all these years, she could feel everything—when the mailman arrived, when her next-door neighbors slammed a door. She knew the sounds and shutters of the house so well she could acutely sense the smallest disturbance. She tossed out the burnt toast and tightened the sash of her threadbare sky-blue silk robe. She spit into her palms, flattened out her static-challenged bob, and quickly applied a subtle lipstick to brighten up her face. Then she made her way through the house, her little dog Gigi weaving underfoot.

Stacks of empty boxes filled up the front hall and were scattered throughout the house—Sonya had seen to that—but Millie had yet to pack anything into them. With a slippered foot she kicked several boxes aside as she went to answer the front door. A blast of late-September heat filled the foyer as she opened it, followed by a waft of the noxious odor from ginkgo fruit falling from the trees up and down the block. Those trees would outlive them all, even the skinny girl standing on the stoop in front of her.

"Good morning to you," she said. "What a lovely surprise." Sally didn't look much like Sonya and Millie was grateful for that, but it was a little unsettling how much she looked like the great-grandmother she was named for, all long necked and sapphire eyed and willowy and graceful beyond her years. It was a fact that Sonya so often liked to point out, how wonderful it was that her daughter had inherited the physical traits of the once-famous forebear she herself had never known.

"I didn't even ring the bell," Sally said as she walked inside. "How did you know I was here?"

"Maybe I'm psychic." Millie winked and quickly shut the door to lock in what cool air she could, the air conditioners being too weak and expensive to run at full tilt.

"No, for real," the girl insisted. "How did you know? Did the monitor sound? Did my mom tell you I was coming?"

"No," Millie said. "It did not. I never turn that thing on. And, no, your mother did not alert me to this wonderful treat. I just knew you were here. Perhaps we are entangled like that."

"What does that mean?" Sally asked, crossing her arms and looking squarely at her grandmother.

Millie wondered what her granddaughter saw. Did she seem dreadfully old, or even old-fashioned? She was wearing a robe, after all. Nobody did that anymore. But her hair was completely white, and while she took some pride in how healthy and, dare she say, stylish it was once the static died down, her coiffed hairdo certainly did not turn back time.

"Do you mean all messed up like my hair gets sometimes?" Sally pressed. Her nature, like that of her great-grandmother, was extroverted and inquisitive, with an assertiveness that made her appear older than she was.

"No, that's just *tangled*," Millie said with a warm smile. "I was just joking, dear, but I suppose saying we are entangled means we are able to influence each other's actions, even when we aren't physically touching. We are connected to each other."

"That makes no sense."

"No, it does. Have you heard of entanglement theory?" Millie asked, although of course the girl hadn't. She was only in fifth or sixth grade; Millie wasn't sure which she had just started or ended. She had a lot to learn about her granddaughter. "It's physics. It has to do with separate objects that are not touching one another but are able to change or influence each other. Just something I learned in college a long time ago."

Millie was enjoying herself, trying to impress this perceptive child, but the truth was, it didn't take psychic powers or higher-level physics for her to know that someone was at the door.

Sally kicked off her sandals.

Her mother must have told her that grandmother preferred that people not wear shoes in the house.

"So tell me," Millie said. "To what do I owe this honor?"

"My mom said I could come," Sally said, and Millie didn't ask anything else. She was thrilled that Sally had come to visit her unchaperoned, even though she guessed that her granddaughter had been sent to inspire her to move things along, to fan her sympathies and soften her stance. Millie was pleased that instead of directly fulfilling that likely command, the girl instead spent much of that morning wandering around the house as if it were a museum, asking about but never touching this thing and that.

Millie padded behind her, more like a puppy than a proprietor, content to watch her granddaughter move about the creaky old house. She followed Sally into the formal living room—the Yellow Room, as she liked to refer to it—pushing aside the faded gold-brocade curtains to allow in some light before she settled on an upholstered chair to watch her granddaughter poke around.

Sally twisted her long blond braid, her thin fingers moving nonstop as her eyes scanned the faded wallpaper. She seemed unnerved by the stiff formality of the space. Or maybe she was unnerved by the looming presence of the grandmother she barely knew, despite the fact that the little girl lived in a small apartment building only two miles away. Millie preferred to think it was the former.

"Do you ever use this room?" the girl asked, head tilted back to take in the dusty chandelier that dripped crystals over the center of the room.

"Not really."

"Yeah, I wouldn't. It's sort of creepy."

"Why do you say that?"

"It's like it isn't a real place, you know? It kind of reminds me of that book about the kids who sleep over in the museum."

"*From The Mixed-Up Files of Mrs. Basil E. Frankweiler?*" It had been one of Millie's favorite books when she was a kid, and she had sent her granddaughter her own dog-eared childhood copy for her last birthday, even though she didn't think the girl would be interested in it. Nobody read books anymore. "Did you read it?"

"Yeah. It was really cool. Was that a real museum? Did you ever go there?"

In the book, two kids spend the night inside New York's Metropolitan Museum of Art, bathing in the water fountain and sleeping on an antique four-poster bed. When Millie was a child herself, barely ten years of age, her mother took her to the museum on occasion, even letting her skip school from time to time. New York City offered a better education than any school could ever provide, her mother used to say, tasking an assistant to watch her daughter during the taping of the show and then meeting up with them on the steps of the Met, where they would pick just one room to explore. Over the next few years they progressed from the old furniture and the suits of armor to the great Masters and special exhibits. The last time they went was a couple of years before Sally Fletcher's death. They went to see an exhibit of work by the Hungarian photographer André Kertész. Years later, when every other dorm room at her college was papered with cheap reproductions of Ansel Adams landscapes, Millie—then called Emilia—hung a poster from that exhibit featuring an image of a fork resting on a plate.

"I did go there," Millie told her granddaughter. "Your great-grandmother and I went there a lot when I was young. At least once a year. I'm sorry I can't take you."

The Met had closed down long before the second Sally was born. Along with books, museums were largely a thing of the past. The rising heat and humidity levels made it too expensive to maintain the collections; museums were shuttering around the world. Even the National Mall, once replete with venerable art institutions, was now mostly a private lake, the upper floors of the limestone palaces serving as waterfront homes.

All of this made the old Fletcher family home, which was close to the highest point in the city, more valuable than most. Even decades after downtown areas had started to close and some of the lower elevation Metro stations started shuttering, the basements on Brandywine Street had yet to flood.

"Don't be so selfish," her daughter had admonished her a few weeks before. "You know that Sally and I need a more comfortable place to live."

"And I don't?" Millie responded. "I have told you, Sonya, that you and Sally are most welcome to move in with me, but I am not going to move out."

Despite her offer, Millie knew full well that they would be at each other's throats half the time if they dared share a roof.

Which brings Millie back to the china. Sally the Second walked over to the corner and asked why the pretty dishes were stacked in the dust-coated glass cabinet.

"They were my mother's," Millie said, as if that explained anything. "I never use them."

"What's the point of having them if you don't use them?" Sally stepped closer to get a better look through the glass.

"Do you want them?" Millie asked, a little sharply. She couldn't help but wonder if Sonya had put Sally up to itemizing her inheritance as she snooped around the house. But Millie would have happily given the plates to Sally, she knew that. All she had to do was ask.

"No, that's not what I meant. They're pretty. You should use them."

"For what? I never have company."

"I'm here."

That was true. Sally was there.

"In that case, how about we take them out?"

The cabinet door was sealed tight from years of disuse and it took them a few minutes to pry it open with one of Sally's barrettes.

"Like a sword in a stone." Millie laughed. "I guess these must all be yours, then."

"What?"

"Don't you know that story, dear? Only the rightful ruler can pull the sword out of the stone. The kingdom is yours." She made a sweeping gesture. "My kingdom for a hug."

The girl regarded her grandmother with a bemused expression, leaving Millie with her arms awkwardly outstretched.

Millie sighed deeply, dropping them. "How about a tea party instead?"

The tea party became a Saturday routine for the two of them. They would sit at the kitchen counter, sipping hot beverages out of the fragile cream-colored china cups that had once belonged to Millie's mom. They would talk about Sally's school, her friends, her favorite books. Sally tried to teach her grandmother a few new words of slang. (*Zipper*—to come together. *On a slide*—having a small fight.) Which was all well and good until one morning—this morning, the sixty-first anniversary of the first Sally's death—as she stirred sugar into her cup, Sally confided, "My mom told me that today is the day your mom died."

Millie put her cup down in its saucer. "That's true. Many years ago now."

"Was she nice?"

She and Sally had discussed all manner of things, but they had never touched upon that part of the past. Certainly never that.

Millie hesitated, unsure of how best to respond. She took a deep breath.

"That's a complicated question."

"Why?"

"What has your mother told you about your great-grandmother?"

"Nothing."

"She must have said something."

Sally sank deep into her chair.

"What is it, dear?"

"I don't know," said the girl. "My mom said this house has

too many bad memories for you and she can't understand why you wouldn't want to leave."

"Your mother thinks I should leave so I don't have to face the memory of my own mother?"

Sally shrugged. This was beyond her pay grade.

"Did she tell you to ask me about this today? What did she say?"

The girl winced. Even at her age she knew this was unfair, that this wasn't a conversation she should have to have. "She said if you can't make the decision to move out, she would make it for you. She said you are getting old and it isn't healthy for you to be here."

"From the mouth of babes," Millie muttered. She shook her head. "I'm sorry she asked you to say all of that."

After that, there wasn't much else to say. The girl gave her grandmother a quick hug and got up to go. "I'll see you later," she said, and Millie watched Sally walk out the door, leaving her all alone in the big house, just as she had been for years. Well, there was the dog. There was always a dog. Still, Sonya wasn't entirely wrong. Millie knew she didn't need all of this space just for herself.

But Sonya wasn't entirely right either.

Millie went to the bathroom to splash some water on her face. She looked into the mirror.

She was old, it was true.

She leaned closer, over the sink, as if there might be something to see on the other side of the glass.

"Good lord," she said out loud, pulling at her jowls. And as she did that, as she pulled the loose, wrinkly skin taut across her face, she began to see signs of her long-deceased mom. She'd never thought she looked much like her mother, but she could see a resemblance now in the contours of her cheeks and the outline of her jaw.

Millie wondered what her mother would say about this decision. Should she stay put or move out? She wasn't sure either way. But she was sure of one thing, and that was that she looked better when she tightened her skin and did up her hair. Perhaps if she looked more like her once-elegant mother instead of a washed-up old woman, Sonya wouldn't be so quick to throw her out. Women like her mother would never wind up in an old-age home.

Now, however many hours later, fresh from her first set of toxic injections, her skin less creased and less mobile than it had been in years, her un-furrowed brow smooth as silk, she leans forward to let her younger selves study her face.

Em touches Millie's face and then she touches her own. She looks over at me. I raise a sympathetic eyebrow.

"Yeah," I say. "It's pretty inevitable, no matter what you do. Aging."

"Better than the alternative," says Millie.

Em isn't so sure. She can't imagine that her mother would have ever been okay with getting old. She would definitely have preferred to be remembered just as she was, just as I (and Em and Millie) always do. Almost always.

19

Daydream Believer: Emilia

I've had a recurring dream about my mother for most of my life, ever since the car crash. I am standing on a beach of smooth black pebbles, looking out toward the horizon. The pebbles underfoot feel like the floor of a shower in an upscale hotel, cool on the soles of my feet, as if the rocks had some sort of curative power. But in the dream, they don't; they're just there, making their presence known, screaming to mean something the way things do in dreams, but I can never figure out what.

Ahead of me, there is nothing.

The water is smooth and the horizon is far. I read somewhere that a person can see two and a half miles on a clear day. So that's how far the horizon must be in my dream. Two and a half miles to the end of the earth.

In the dream, the temperature is not always the same. Sometimes it is crisp, sometimes it is humid and hot, but that is something I have chalked up to the room temperature of wherever I happen to be sleeping (lately, I've been factoring perimenopause into the equation as well). The heat, or lack of it, has no symbolic significance that I can discern.

What is significant, however, is that while I am standing there, staring out over the placid expanse of water, I know I am not alone.

I turn to my left and where a moment before there was nothing, now there is the thick trunk of a half-dead ginkgo tree emerging from the shoreline. The top half has been sheared off as if struck by lightning, but a crooked limb protrudes from one side, like a fractured bone. There is something simultaneously grotesque and hopeful about this mutant limb, with its yellowed fan-shaped leaves and the thick, tubular basal chichi roots reaching down from the branch like it is trying to brace against coastal winds. As I move to get a closer look, an enormous tsunami-like wave comes crashing over me. Plunged beneath the water, I see dark bubbles and start to panic. Lungs bursting, I fight to get to the surface, to get a mouthful of air. When I break free, gasping, I notice a slender blond woman beside the tree staring out over the water, a hand shading her eyes as if she is looking for someone or something.

The woman, my mother, isn't aware of me. Before I can call for her, however, another wave descends and I am pulled again beneath the surface.

I've had the dream so many times that over the years I have trained myself to wake up before the moment when I begin to drown, but no matter how quickly I can break free, I always wake up gasping for breath.

That in and of itself wasn't such a big deal, until I had to deal with having another person sleeping next to me.

The first time was the worst. I had somehow fallen asleep nestled on the floor of a large coat closet. I shot up, panting, and it took a moment to even remember where I was. Alpha Epsilon Pi—I had gone to the Purim party they were hosting, which sounded wholesome enough, but I was no fool. A costume party was a costume party, and a frat was a frat. Did I honestly expect I would end up anyplace else? No. But I didn't expect this.

"Are you okay?" A young man sat next to me, slumped over a mound of winter jackets. I couldn't recall his name, but he knew mine. "Emilia, are you okay?"

Through the partially open closet door, I could hear the pounding bass of the Beastie Boys from the floor below. The party was still in full swing.

"What?" I asked. "Oh." I pushed myself away from this guy, kicking some coats in my wake. *What happened?* I kept asking myself. *Who was this guy?*

"Are you okay? You were screaming and then you woke up all upset."

Of course I was upset. And who the fuck was he? And then it hit me. Right. Joel. From my Russian class. Now I remembered. I had let this happen. I always let this happen. But he seemed nice enough. I exhaled loudly.

"I should go."

"No, wait." He grabbed my wrist.

"Really?" I said, eyebrow arched.

He didn't let go. "Really. You were screaming."

"I know that."

Joel let go. "Sorry."

He wasn't bad-looking, this Joel guy. Broad shoulders, a little stocky, a thick head of curly blond hair. But he wasn't my type. Nobody was my type. Or was it the other way around? Maybe I was nobody's type.

"Did we?" I asked, because I wasn't sure. My clothing was all where it was supposed to be. More or less.

Joel looked confused. "Did we what?"

"Are you serious?"

"You don't remember?"

"I had a few drinks."

Joel looked at me. There wasn't anything about me that was dramatically appealing one way or another. I was very thin. I did have nice eyebrows. But now I know there was something else that he liked—I was a mystery.

"No. We just talked."

"We talked?"

"In Russian."

I laughed. We were only a couple of months into the introductory class. I had enrolled in it because I wanted to read *Anna Karenina* in the original someday. "It must have been a deep conversation."

"Very. You know, Soviet nuclear testing, Dostoevsky. Typical stuff."

"Right." I relaxed.

"So what was that about?"

"Dostoevsky?"

"No. Your dream. Do you remember?"

"No," I lied.

"You were quite upset. I woke up because you were kicking my legs."

I said nothing.

"You were screaming."

"Are you done?"

"Sorry, I just—"

"I should go."

"I was just trying to—"

"Well, don't try," I said, shrugging into my coat. "See you in class." I took off on my so-called walk of shame, even if there wasn't actually anything to be ashamed about. Not this time.

It would be a more fairytale-like wrap to say that after that, we met again, we kissed, and then we lived happily ever after. But no, it wasn't so simple. And years later, whenever the dream occurred, Joel had a better handle on what to say. He said nothing. He turned on his side and went back to sleep.

The New York Times

Wedding Announcement

Emilia E. Fletcher, Joel S. Gregory

Emilia Elizabeth Fletcher, the daughter of Samuel K. Fletcher and the late Sally L. Fletcher of Washington, DC, was married last evening to Joel Scott Gregory, son of Linda H. Gregory and the late Dr. Wallace M. Gregory. Crystal Mayfair, an associate judge at Eastern Maryland District Court, officiated at the Fletcher family vacation home in Bay View, Maryland.

The bride, 32, is an associate producer for the WBS News program *Sunrise America*, based in Washington, DC. She transferred from Tufts University to Columbia University, from which she graduated.

The bride's mother was host of *Sunrise America* until her death in 1986. The bride's father is a novelist.

The groom, also 32, is an attorney with Pointer, Fitch, and McKinley, a law firm in Washington, DC, which specializes in immigration and civil rights. The groom's father was a law professor at New York University until his death in 2001. The groom's mother teaches kindergarten at the Ethical Culture School in Manhattan.

The couple first met at Tufts University in 1988, but they reconnected while separately attending the wedding of a mutual friend last summer.

20

Tick-Tock: Emilia

October 12
6:03 p.m.
Friendship Heights Metro
Washington, DC

Time keeps ticking forward the way it always does, but Em, Millie, and I remain at an impasse. After more hours than I care to count, there is just so little that seems to give.

"Jesus, it's getting hot in here," I say, partly because I want to change the topic and partly because it's true. There is sweat pooling under the wires of my bra.

I tug at my top. "Do you guys mind if I take this thing off?"

"Why on earth would we mind?" Millie asks, although she says she has no intention of removing her own top, hot though she is. She's seventy-seven years old, for Pete's sake. She doesn't want her young selves to have to see *that*. But she happily watches me disrobe down to my dingy old bra.

"I looked good back then," Millie murmurs, as if talking to herself. "I wish I'd had a better sense of that. All I ever saw were the flaws—the dimpled thighs, the loosening skin under my arms, the—"

"Okay, I get it. I get it," I say, feeling grateful that Millie decided not to disrobe. It would probably kill me to get an advanced peek at what happens later, to see how different I will look in decades to come. When does it all start to unravel? Will it matter if I start to go to the gym more?

I drape my top onto the pile of clothing I have pulled out of the shopping bags.

"Can I see that?" Millie asks, pointing at a pale lavender scarf sticking out from under the mound. "I think I may still have that."

I pull out the sheer square of silky fabric. It has a subtle batik design and I had been thinking Sonya might like it, though I wasn't sure for what. I'd bought it anyway, just in case. "Here." I toss it to Millie, but it is like trying to throw a feather and it wafts to the floor.

When I lean over to retrieve the scarf, something sharp jabs into my palm. "Fuck! What was that?" A dark line of blood trickles from just below my thumb as I discover my metal nail file on the ground.

"I'm guessing neither of you has a Band-Aid," I say, as blood drips toward my wrist.

"I have a scar in that same spot," Millie says, holding out her palm. "How strange. I could never recall where I got it. It's just something I've had for a long time."

"Jesus," Em pipes in. "That's fucking creepy." She pushes herself onto her knees to reach the scarf. "Here," she says, passing it to me. "Wrap it around your hand to stop the bleeding."

"Aren't you the Girl Scout?" I say with a sly grin.

"Ha, ha," says Em, because as inside jokes go, it's not that funny; we all know that our experience with the Scouts had been a total failure. In fifth grade, Amy and I were asked to leave our troop because we ate more cookies than we sold. My parents, luckily, were mostly amused. "Screw them," my mother said. "We can bake our own cookies and hold a bake sale ourselves. Donate to a charity of your choosing." It was a fine idea, even if it never happened. Still, Amy and I were happy to have Saturday afternoons back to ourselves.

"It's okay," I say. "I have this." I blot my hand on the camisole I have just taken off. "It's cotton, so it's probably more absorbent."

"Here," Em says, tossing the scarf back toward Millie. "Try again."

Just as Millie reaches to grab it, the light—again—snaps off and we are plunged into darkness.

"So much for getting a better look," Millie says. "Oh my, it smells like a department store. I don't think I've been inside one of those in over twenty-five years."

"I can see how that happens," I say. "I have a terrible Amazon Prime addiction."

"It gets worse," says Millie.

"What are you talking about?" asks Em. "Actually, never mind. I don't care."

"Okay," I say.

"Okay," says Em, and that is the last thing she says until— after a good half hour of staring into the dark while Millie and I blather on about how we order pet food and toilet paper and crap like that—she mutters that she is bored out of her fucking skull.

"Boredom is a sign of a lazy mind, Em," I say in a singsong voice. It is one of those grating things our mother used to say.

"Very funny."

"It's a valid point," says Millie.

"So what do you suggest, then, oh wise sage?" asks Em. "You have a game to play or something? Because I am so done with listening to you guys talk about how you stock your pantries."

"No need to get sassy, young lady," says Millie.

"No need to get preachy either."

"A game is a good idea," I say, trying to diffuse the latest swirl of tension I seem to have unleashed. "Let's do that."

"Like what?"

"Twenty questions?"

"There's more like a thousand."

"Let's start with twenty."

"You first."

'Fine." I think for a minute. Nothing good comes to mind. "Oh, fuck it, let's do something else."

"How about this?" Millie suggests. "If this weren't an elevator, where else could we be?"

"In a closet?"

"Talk about a lazy mind," says Em.

"Okay, Em, why don't you take a stab."

"Okay." Em ponders the idea. "Let's pretend we are at the beach. But it's a cloudy night and we can't even see the stars."

"Why would we go to the beach on a cloudy night?"

"We are waiting for the sun to rise," Em says. Which it does, in a fashion. The hot white light flickers back on, and it is suddenly bearing down upon us with such ferocity that it may as well be the heat source at the center of the solar system.

"And there you have it," Em says. She stretches out flat on her back, pretending to sunbathe. "Hmm, that feels nice."

"Just a day at the beach," I say, simultaneously irritated and amused. I did love to sunbathe, once upon a time. Amy and I used to slather each other in baby oil and hold aluminum trays under our chins. How little we knew. How happy I felt. Looking over at Em, I am mildly envious of her proximity to a more innocent time. But look at her.

Jesus.

She is so skinny. Her hip bones jut up through her jeans and her sweatshirt dips into the concavity of her stomach. I used to be so proud about that. Now I just wish I could give Em some food.

"I wish it smelled like coconuts," Em says, her eyes still closed. "You got any Coppertone in that bag of yours?"

"I don't think you are at risk of getting a sunburn in here," says Millie.

"I'm just joking. You know? Trying to relax? I recommend it. Hey, maybe if we can fall asleep, when we wake up this will all have been just another bad dream."

"No mutant ginkgo trees in this one," I say, shielding my eyes with my hand as if I were looking for a horizon.

"Not much in the way of water either," says Millie.

"Wait." Em sits up. "You guys have that dream too?"

"Quite often," I say, and Millie says, "I do as well."

"With Mom and the tree and the wave?"

"Is there another?" I ask. "I've had the same dream for the last thirty-odd years. Sometimes it comes almost every night, and then I don't have it for months."

"The dream changes," says Millie. "Sometimes, instead of our mother, I see Joel."

"Really?" I ask. That is surprising. "Since when?"

"Since a few decades ago."

"Who's Joel?" Em asks, and Millie and I look at each other, unsure of what to say. It's funny how this far into our confinement he hasn't even come up, we've all been so wrapped up in the past.

"My husband," I say as Millie says, "My ex-husband" at the same exact time.

"What?" I ask, taken aback.

"What does he look like? Where did you meet?" Em asks, apparently less interested in the trajectory of the marriage than the fact that there is one at all.

"What do you mean, ex?" I ask indignantly.

"What did you think would happen?" asks Millie.

"Not that."

"Maybe it won't happen like that for you. What do I know?" Millie lifts her palms up and shrugs. "But that's certainly how it happened for me."

"But we've been trying to work things out," I say pleadingly. Then I think about the message Joel left on my phone earlier that day. "Fuck. What should I do?"

"Oh, come on now. It could have been a fairly simple fix. You know as well as I do that you never make room for him."

"That's not true," I protest. "He has plenty of room."

Millie shakes her head. "Those maple saplings will be dead by the time you get home," she says, as if that settles her point.

I am not having it. We wouldn't do that to Sonya. No way.

"But what can I do?" I ask.

"You have a decision to make."

"Wait." Why would this be my decision? "So you're saying you're the one—I'm going to be the one—who decides to split up?"

"That's not what I am saying."

"Okay, what then?"

"I've often thought that I married Joel for the wrong reasons. So I suppose I'm saying that I could have chosen to stay for the right ones."

"Hang on!" Em seems horrified by this tsunami of information. "What wrong reasons?" she asks. "Didn't you love each other?"

"He thought he loved me," Millie explains to Em. "That was better than I could say for myself at the time. I just never fully loved him back. I couldn't. I didn't know how."

"Then why in the world did you marry him?"

"Because," I say, relieving Millie of the interrogation, "he was a nice guy and it felt better than the alternative."

"Which was?"

"Being with myself."

"And here we are." Millie opens her arms in a mock embrace.

"Very funny."

Em isn't having it either. "But you must love him. Why else would you be so upset about things ending?"

I shiver. "I do love him." I've come to love him, I realize. To the best of my abilities, anyway. Isn't that enough?

"But you don't love yourself," Millie says.

I choose not to respond to such insipid psychobabble. I grab one of my shirts off the floor and blow my nose in it so they can't see my face.

Em grabs my wrist. "Maybe it's not too late. You can fix things when we get out."

"Like that's going to happen." I feel as if there is a hole growing in my chest. "I am not sure that we are ever going to get out."

"What do you mean? Someone will come sooner or later,"

says Em. "I'm sure my dad is scared out of his mind by now. There will be a big search. There has to be."

"Even if there were, why would they look here? You usually get on at Tenleytown."

"The daughter of Sally Fletcher, missing?" says Em. "Are you kidding? They'll look everywhere."

"Don't count on it. Anyway, my point is that it can't happen at all."

"What do you mean?"

"What I mean is that we can't leave together, can we? We can't all three exist in the same space and time."

"We seem to be existing here," Em says, but she knows that what I am saying is true. It's one thing to face your past and future in a confined space, but all three in the world at once would make *Back To The Future* seem like the simplest movie concept ever.

"Yes," Millie adds. "We are all here, as clear as day. This isn't a dream."

"It may as well be, though," says Em. "Whatever happens, nobody will ever believe it anyway."

"Well, we should be used to that by now," I say. "It certainly won't be the first time nobody believes us about what happened inside of a dark metal box."

21

Morning Edition, Part 4: Emilia

October 12, 2017
9:30 a.m.
Brandywine Street, NW
Washington, DC

I sat on my front stoop waiting for the Uber driver, trying not to look at the burlap-covered root balls of the maple saplings lying in the front yard. At least they weren't ginkgo trees; I could give Joel that. While my house might be blessedly free of ginkgo, the sun was filtering through the yellow fan-shaped leaves that remained on the block; it was pretty enough, but even the gentlest breeze would rain rotten-smelling ginkgo fruit down on the hoods of parked cars, across the sidewalk, and into the street. When a car drove down the road, it crushed the fallen fruit into a sticky yellow paste. Every year the trees grew in size and the fruitful bounty multiplied. Neighbors tried to sweep the putrid fruit into the drain, but it was a Sisyphean effort. I imagined that by the time I died they would need to bring out snowplows to clear the street of its wretched blanket of pulp.

In the battle between me and the ginkgo trees, these unstoppable trees will always win. Scientists study them because they seem to resist climate change more than most. Ginkgo trees are so fucking resilient that more than a hundred of them survived the atomic bombing of Hiroshima, and some of those are still alive today. They are the oldest living fossil, for God's sake, dating back more than two hundred million years.

So sure. Fine. These trees are an amazing specimen—that, I could admit. Olfactory issues of the fruiting females aside, the branches and leaves created a beautiful canopy, and each year, late in the fall, the leaves turn a brilliant yellow, a hue so golden it draws tourists all the way up from the National Mall.

While the rest of the street looked like a cathedral, our front yard offered a barren gap. Joel often complained that it was selfish of me and my father to have had that ginkgo tree taken down all those decades ago, that a few months of stench was nothing compared to the trees' majesty. Sometimes I wondered if the tree in my dream had something to do with that, with killing something beautiful.

Maybe.

There was the obvious drowning-means-being-overwhelmed thing, and the not-being-able-to-connect-with-my-mother thing—those things I had tried to talk about with a number of therapists over the years. But my mother appearing next to that half-dead, half-immortal ginkgo tree? That part I couldn't figure out.

I tapped on the Uber app and watched as a cartoon car turned down Reno off Nebraska, and then headed north instead of south. "Are you kidding me?" I said aloud. It wasn't as if my house was on some strange cul-de-sac or an obscure side street. The streets around my house were laid out in a grid, alphabetically ordered. Did the driver not know how to read?

"Fuck it," I said and began to walk down the street, scrupulously avoiding the noxious yellow pulp that blanketed the street.

Halfway to Wisconsin Avenue, I heard my phone bleat like a sheep, a ringtone I had assigned to Joel because of his curly hair. By the time I fished my phone out of my bag, it had gone to voicemail.

I tried to call Joel back, but he didn't answer. I would just have to wait until he finished recording whatever it was that he wanted to say.

iPhone Transcription Beta

Hey I feel ya. Um. It's jewel. Obviously. Look,
I shouldn't say this on a voice message, but I
just need to ____and um later __. I spoke to
____and he thinks it might be a good idea for
us to take some time _____ um and____lawyer and
_____the rest of____talk tonight____um_____
bye.

Was this transcription useful or not useful?

No. It was not fucking useful. Lawyer? What the hell did
that even mean? Things between us were bad, but come on.
I figured it must have just mis-transcribed the word *later*, not
lawyer—until I listened to the recording.

I had no idea how to respond.

I stared at my phone, trying to think of what I wanted to
say, trying to summon the courage to try to call him again, to
challenge him, to curse at him, to beg his forgiveness, to—I
don't even know what—when my phone rang instead.

It wasn't him.

It was the Uber driver wanting to know if I was coming out
soon, so I turned back around, crushing yet another ginkgo
fruit as I spun on my heel. How fucking perfect, I thought,
scraping the bottom of my shoe against the sidewalk before
making my way back toward the house.

22

MIND GAMES: EM

October 12, 1986
12:43 p.m.
Bay Breeze, MD

The car, a present from Em's mother, had cost more than the advance on her father's unfinished novel, one that was already three years overdue. It was a grand gesture—a one-and-a-half-ton shiny red confidence booster complete with five cylinders of raw power to push him ahead. The temporary cardboard license plate was still in place the morning of the crash, that's how new the car was.

This fact sealed her father's story, because in what universe would any parent allow such a green driver to take command of a brand-new Audi that had only just been driven off the lot? It was both a stupid question and a believable refrain. Why would his daughter have been at the wheel? What parent in his or her right mind would have let such an untested driver take control of a pristine, luxurious new automobile? It made no sense.

Except to Em. To Em it made all the sense in the world.

"It was me! It was...my...fault," she cried to the ER tech who was trying to get her to lie down on the stretcher in the back of the ambulance. "Please...let me talk to...the police," she stammered through frozen lips and chattering teeth.

"Where's...my...my...father?" she demanded as the ambulance pulled onto the road. "What happened to my mom? Oh my God!" She tried to grab at the technician's white coat as he held her down. "Where did they take my mom? Where is she? Where did they put her?" Em begged for an answer, but either they didn't hear her or they were simply not paying her any mind. She was just this side of hysterical. The medical technician told her to relax, to lie down. He told her that her father was in another ambulance right behind them. He made no mention of her mother at all.

Em didn't want to lie down, but she strained against the weight of the blankets being piled on top of her.

"The patient is hypothermic," the technician shouted into the radio, alerting the hospital to the incoming patient. "Pulse is weak. Pupils dilated. Irritable. Signs of confusion."

"I am not confused!" Em reached toward the technician, desperate to get his attention, but found she was too tightly tucked in to do even that. "I am not confused!" she repeated. "I am totally clear!" She was practically chanting. "I am not confused! I was driving the car! It's all my fault! I was driving the car!"

"Signs of irritability and confusion," the technician repeated for emphasis. "Shivering. Seems overly animated. Hyperactive."

And then they were at the hospital and the nurse at her bedside in the ER was also refusing to listen.

"You are imagining it, sweetheart," she said in response to Em's ongoing mantra. "I am sure this is all overwhelming. But it was your father driving the car, not you." She brushed Em's hair back from her forehead, tenderly, as a mother might. "Now come on, your temperature is still very low. We need to get you warmed up."

It was true that she was still shaking. Even though she had been stripped of all her clothing and wrapped in scratchy wool blankets with hot water bottles piled on top, Em's temperature was precariously low and her head was starting to throb, as if her skull were too small for her brain.

"I'm going to be sick!" she cried. The nurse handed her a barf bag, and Em took it, retching, as sour green bile poured out of her.

The nurse jotted some things down on a clipboard. "A doctor will be in soon." She handed Em an extra bag just in case.

"Try to calm yourself," she said, and spun off on the heel of her clog.

And then Em was alone, surrounded by sheets draped from curtain rods. She could hear people pacing back and forth in the corridor, one bed rolling by, the next one being rolled in. She heard a commotion coming from the other side of the fabric wall, the sheet wafting toward her as someone brushed against it.

"Fletcher," she heard someone say. "Samuel. Male. Fifty-three."

"Dad?" Em asked in a loud whisper as a bed rolled into the space on the other side of the sheet, the wheels visible in the gap between the cloth and the floor. "Dad, is that you?"

"Is it all right, sir?" someone else asked. Her father must have nodded yes, because the sheets were pushed aside and there he was, prone on a bed in a similar fashion, laden down with piles of those blankets and hot water bottles. He was pale and shaking and he looked incredibly old.

"Em…" he muttered. He tried to extend a hand to reach her, but their beds were too far apart.

"Daddy!" she cried, and, for the first and what would be the last time since the accident, she started to sob. "Daddy! I am so sorry. I am so sorry. It's all my fault. I just…" She spluttered and muttered and sobbed some more. Because she knew they were there because of a series of decisions she would forever regret. If she hadn't gone to the party, if she hadn't let Christopher push her head down, if none of that had happened, they wouldn't be here. They wouldn't have had the pity party for their pathetic little girl and let her drive the car.

Et matricides. Matricide. She had just learned the word in Latin class and it flitted into her mind. That is what it was. She had killed her mother, and there was no convincing her otherwise.

Her father tried to calm her down, to shush her, to say it's okay in the way that parents do even when it's not. It's not your fault, he insisted. You didn't do anything wrong.

This was very much the wrong thing to say.

"You know it was me. Why do you keep saying that?" she demanded.

"No. No, Em. I was the one who lost control of the car," he insisted over and over so many times Em thought he might actually believe that.

She screamed. Growled really. It was a feral cry. She had killed her mother and now her father was going mad.

The nurse pulled back the curtain at the foot of her bed. "Is everything okay?" Em heard her ask. "Room 10!" the nurse called over her shoulder. "Code violet!" And suddenly an army cloaked in white and shielded by clipboards materialized at her side.

The next thing Em knew, she was being pushed down deeper into the bed as even more blankets were added to the heap, as if that might keep her in place.

"She's hyperventilating," someone said.

"Hypothermic delusion," said someone else.

"Psychiatric consult recommended," another person yelled to someone else down the hall.

PSYCHIATRIC INTAKE FORM
Patient: Emilia Fletcher
DOB: April 26, 1969
Today's Date: October 22, 1986

Please answer these questions to the best of your ability.

What is the main problem for which you are hoping to get help?

I KILLED MY MOTHER BUT NOBODY BELIEVES ME.

When did it start?

THE DAY I KILLED HER.

Has your appetite, weight, or eating patterns changed since this happened?

WHAT DO YOU THINK? I KILLED MY MOTHER, FOR GOD'S SAKE. AND NOBODY BELIEVES ME. I THINK I HAVE A GOOD APPETITE CONSIDERING THAT. ANYWAY, TAKE A LOOK AT ME. I LOOK LIKE SHIT.

Have your sleeping patterns changed since this happened?

CAN I LEAVE NOW? I DON'T SEE HOW THIS IS HELPFUL.

Observations, to be filled in by clinician.

Patient presents as a normal, adolescent girl. Appropriate eye contact, able to engage in standard introductory exchanges, with a sullen and slightly angry affect to be expected after the recent loss of a parent. She was brought to the consultation by her father, who is concerned about her fixation on guilt after her mother's tragic death. The girl insists that she was at fault for the death, although father and police report that she was not the one driving the car at the time of the accident.

After speaking at length with the father, and
after speaking with the girl, it is my opinion
that she is suffering from both a dissociative
disorder and FMS (False Memory Syndrome), due
to the complicated relationship she had with
her mother prior to the accident. The fact that
her mother's overtures were rejected by the
girl just prior to the accident has distorted
her memory of what actually occurred. Ongoing
psychotherapy is recommended. A sedative med-
ication might be useful to help with agitation
and sleep disruptions.

23

October 12
6:48 p.m.
Friendship Heights Metro
Washington, DC

In the elevator, the light flickers back and forth and time drips forward like a molasses spill, slow and sticky. A moment of recall is followed by an aggressive rebuttal. A kind overture by one of us is slapped into silence by another as we each stew in our time-adjusted memories.

"They didn't actually send us to the psych ward that day," I say. "I am pretty sure I remember that correctly."

"You don't. Obviously," Em snaps. "They were talking about doing a lobotomy when they were pushing the stretcher through the halls. I would think you would remember that?"

"Don't be ridiculous. Nobody ever suggested we get a lobotomy. That wasn't even something people did back then."

"I heard it. That's what they said."

I turn to Millie for reinforcement.

She nods for my sake but keeps her eyes on Em. "They were probably talking about someone else, dear. Although I don't recall that either. Regardless, if someone did say something about a lobotomy, it wasn't about us. No need to embellish the story," she says, referring, I am sure, to our lifelong penchant for doing just that.

"You do both remember being stabbed by that nurse, don't you?" Em demands.

"Yes, I do," I say. "She had to insert an IV. But my memory is fairly blurry after that."

"That's because you had a concussion," says Em. "You don't remember it clearly."

"That's because it was a long time ago," says Millie.

"Whatever. Think what you want. It doesn't matter."

"But it does matter," I say. "It matters how we remember things. Isn't this"—I mime the stirring of a pot—"why we are here?"

"This?" Em says, mimicking me rather aggressively. She may as well stick out her tongue, she is becoming so petulant.

"Yes, Em. This. I mean, it is the anniversary of Mom's death, for God's sake. And here we are, all together. Whether this is hell or just some horrifically bad dream, it's the only thing that makes sense."

"Well, maybe I don't want to grapple anymore," Em says, wrapping her arms tightly across her chest. "This is bullshit. We've been here for hours and nothing has changed."

As if on cue, like the fading out of a movie scene or the dropping of a curtain, the light once again goes off and the darkness holds steady.

"Fuck!" Em shouts in frustration. She slaps the wall and the sound reverberates across the space in an undulating, palpable wave.

"Fuck, indeed," I say softly.

Then, for a few minutes, we are quiet, but frustration is mounting and, as the loud grumbles from Em's corner attest, hunger is too. She sighs audibly. "Do either of you have any-thing to eat?"

I know there is the stale Kind bar in my bag, but that's hardly enough to go around. Plus, now my nausea has subsided and I could stand to eat something myself. For a brief moment I think that maybe in the dark the other two won't notice if I eat it, but I think again as I grope around in my bag and can't smother the sound of the crinkling wrapper. I cringe. "I found something," I confess. I tear off the plastic and break the bar in half. I've gone this long without eating; I can wait a little longer. Hopefully it won't be too much longer. "Here." I briefly turn on the flashlight of my phone so I can see them long enough to pass it to them.

"None for you?" Millie asks before putting it in her mouth.

"I'm fine," I lie, and turn off the light.

It would be nice if this breaking of bread, so to speak, broke the tension. But it doesn't. When the light finally flickers back on—first with a teasing stutter of light and then finally holding steady—I am sitting in a half-lotus position trying to channel some strength, Millie is sagging against the wall, and Em has taken to sulking in her corner with her back turned to us.

"Em, things will get better. I promise," I say, because it feels like the right thing to say.

"Bullshit," Em mumbles back. Good God, I can't believe I was ever this obnoxious.

"You do realize how tiresome this behavior of yours is, don't you?" I say. "Or, I guess I should say, you *will* realize it. Look, it is stupid to stew in this narcissistic cycle you are in. Shouldering all the blame is a fairly unproductive endeavor, especially if no one believes you."

Em doesn't respond. I know why and immediately feel stupid for saying what I just said. She's already had this conversation countless times in the past year. There isn't a therapist alive who wouldn't say the same thing that I just said, but that doesn't necessarily make it true.

"Some might say it's also destructive," Millie weighs in. "Emilia, you'd do well to listen to your own advice."

There is a dig here, I know, but I am not sure exactly what Millie is getting at.

"Are you trying to pick a fight with me too?" I ask. Good grief, am I getting tired of this. Seven-plus hours in, it would be nice if the three of us could hold a steadier peace.

"Not at all. I'm just saying that Em isn't the only one of us who could use some course correcting. You can't deny that your inability to come to terms with your mother's death is a fairly constant feature in your life. It does cast a shadow, does it not?"

"I see. So you've got it all figured out, then?" I say, wanting but not wanting to ask for more details about what will happen between me and Joel.

Millie grins and gently wobbles her head, and I wonder for a moment if she has early-stage Parkinson's, but she quickly makes it clear that the gesture is simply condescending, not afflicted. "No, not entirely. But it would stand to reason that I have more perspective. Maybe listening to your elder could serve you well once in a while?"

"Could you both please shut up?" Em blurts out. "I have a fucking headache."

"Oh, you have a headache?" I have to restrain myself from laughing. "Just wait."

"Truer words, my dear... But I will say, Emilia isn't wrong, Em. Your life isn't entirely the tableau of purgatory that you think it is. Or that you think it should be. It wasn't before Mom's death, and it doesn't have to be after." She looks over to me for backup. "Show her."

"Show her what?"

"Just give me your phone."

I do as I am told, and, not surprisingly, when Millie presses her thumb onto the start button, her fingerprint registers and the screen glows to life.

"Here," she says. She pulls herself up off the ground and goes over to Em, shoving the phone in front of her face. "It's not all bad."

Em takes the phone, of course. She is not immune to the magnetic pull of all those shiny ones and zeros. She spends a few minutes with it, swiping this and tapping on that, and I can feel the tension dissipating.

"This is so..." she says, still not turning around. She holds the phone up over her head so Millie and I can both see the screen. "Is this your daughter?"

It is.

Seeing the images of Sonya moving in that Harry Potter

photographic way, a two-second dance into steadiness, makes me happy for a moment. A slice of a moment really, until the worry starts to seep in. Where is she now? Did she get dinner? Did she call Joel? Is she concerned that I am still not home?

"That was taken a few years ago," I say, refocusing on the past—Em has paused on a photo of a nine-year-old Sonya, taken from behind. She is standing in front of the Lincoln Memorial looking out over the mall, her long blond hair frizzed out from the summer heat. With one hand on a hip and the other pointing to the sky, she looks like a disco queen giving a sassy speech from the steps. "We played tourist that day. Sonya's hair is shorter now. And darker."

"Sonya," Millie says with a nostalgic tinge in her voice. "We named her after the girl in *Crime and Punishment*." She laughs. "We were a touch pretentious like that."

"True," I have to concede. "But it fits her, don't you think?"

"Maybe. Things change," Millie says.

"What do you mean?"

"She didn't stay so saintly. You'll see."

I should want to ask more, but I don't. I don't want to know if my once sweet, gentle girl becomes, well, not that. And as much as I know that Millie is right, that I still might have a chance for a course correction, it feels both overwhelming and presumptuous to think that I could even have a modicum of power to influence the woman that Sonya will become. She is her own person, isn't she? Aren't we all?

But it's not that simple. Just look at the three of us sitting in here.

Em is still swiping away, too absorbed in the device, mesmerized by her future daughter. I look over her shoulder, admiring the image of the cherubic two-year-old Sonya on the screen, her light hair wisped around her face in a sunlit halo, her eyes a brilliant blue with the reflection of the pool.

"I can't believe she's in middle school now," I say. "That photo feels like a million years ago."

Millie gives me a sympathetic nod.

"That's crazy," says Em.

"Life speeds up."

"No, I mean seeing her at the pool. Do you still go there? To Bay Breeze?"

"Can I see?" asks Millie.

Em holds the screen up higher for Millie to see better, and the old woman sighs heavily.

"What's wrong?"

"Nothing. It's just that it was such a beautiful place back then," Millie explains. "It was so lush. So green. I haven't seen anything like that for a long time."

I haven't either. At least, I haven't seen the house. We sold the property just a few months after this photo was taken, after my father died. I do miss the country house, though—there are plenty of good memories mixed up with the bad: I miss the clean chlorine scent that competed with the wildflowers just behind the wooden fence; the periodic complaints of the cows next door; the plates of freshly cut melon that my mother would bring to the side of the pool so I could nosh on something without having to get off the raft.

24

Poolside Attractions: Em

Early 1980s
Bay Breeze, MD

To be clear, it wasn't just any old melon plate. Em's mother had never been one for straightforward presentations. No, in this case, for example, the honeydew slices formed the petals of what was intended to look like a floral arrangement; in the center, there was a perfect circle of raspberries, with one plump strawberry (but never a cherry) on top. That was her way.

"You never know who might show up," her mother would often say when Em was young, as if somebody might just happen to swing by their country house unannounced, traveling more than two hours and a confusing maze of country roads away from DC.

The house itself wasn't intended for show, and on the rare occasions when someone did stop by, her mother was always reluctant to invite them inside. But this is why Em loved it there, precisely because it wasn't for show. It was for them. The lovingly arranged fruit was just for them. It was for them to put their feet up on the thick pine coffee table, for them to sink into the deep couch in front of the fire, for them to leave a glass on the counter and not worry about a snide comment or slight. There, Em could come in through the front door whenever she pleased.

It wasn't like that in DC. In DC, for example, when she was little, she had been trained to enter through the mudroom at the back of the house, hang up her backpack, and line up her shoes. If Ruby, the housekeeper, was in a good mood, Em would hear her humming away in the kitchen, and it was a signal for Em that she could relax. But if she walked in and saw Ruby looking stern, furiously chopping or baking or mixing, laying out elegant canapés or arranging a floral display, then Em knew she was in for a bad afternoon. In that case, she would try to slip up the back stairs, in stocking feet, like a prowler. It rarely worked.

"Emilia!" her mother would call in a singsong chirp, using her full name, not her nickname. Em knew this meant she had a guest. A guest Em would need to perform for and impress.

When Em was younger, she would reluctantly answer the call. She would reverse course and walk back through the kitchen, past the small nook with the built-in bench where she ate most of her meals, past the dining room with the table perpetually primed for a party with its twelve velvet-cushioned chairs circling around as if they were the rapt audience of the fresh floral centerpiece, through the foyer with the sky-high ceiling from which hung a chandelier that, at least according to her mother, had once belonged to Jackie Kennedy, and into the sitting room—to call it a living room would suggest a place for more animated lifeforms—where her mother would be chatting with this or that person, someone that Emilia was supposed to know, whose presence was supposed to impress.

Em would enter the yellow sitting room (wallpaper with pale yellow birds, curtains of golden yellow silk, upholstery that should have by no means gone as many years as it had without getting stained), smiling as she had been taught, looking straight into each visitor's eyes for at least a count of three, and then introducing herself with a forced trill of pleasure, as if there were nothing in the world she would rather be doing at the moment than making the acquaintance of some bloated secretary of this or director of that.

But not by the pool at the country house. There Em didn't have to perform for anyone. She could walk around barefoot most of the time or relax with her nose stuck deep in a book, and she wouldn't have to speak gaily to a single soul. She and her dad would spend large chunks of the summer there, with her mother flitting back and forth, appearing Friday or Saturday nights when it suited her, but then she would arrive, and her presence would be quickly and deeply felt.

There, at least until Em was around the age of the Sonya in the photo at the Lincoln Memorial, her mother would hug her as if making up for lost time (which she was); she'd sit down next to Em, dangling her feet in the pool. She put her reportorial skills to work as they nibbled on the melon, asking Em question after question about her life, her friends, her dreams, not in an annoying way, but in a professional way, in the way of a veteran interviewer who knew exactly how to draw someone out, the kind of way that would make any six-, ten-, or even thirteen-year-old feel special. But here there were no cameras, there was no audience, no need to stand on ceremony, fruit platter aside.

And later, throughout her life, it is when Em thinks about those moments—as a young girl sitting by the pool with her mom, talking (well, answering) until the evening chill would start to settle on her skin and the smell of meat cooking on the grill cut through the chlorinated air to waft their way—it is the memories of those moments that make her miss her mom most, or make her feel even worse, depending on what life stage she is in at the time.

25

A Heavenly Way to Die: Emilia

October 12
8:26 p.m.
Friendship Heights Metro
Washington, DC

Em gives me the phone, waving it with some urgency because she doesn't want to see any more. I don't want her to, either. The low battery warning is starting to blink.

"How about I preserve our memory lane for now," I say, plucking the device away from her.

"Good riddance," Em mutters and falls back into her sulking position, knees to chest, eyes to floor. "Goddamn it, I wish we could turn off that fucking light."

I am getting tired of it too. When it is pitch black, it's unsettling, sure, but right now it's so bright it hurts my eyes, and because of that our circadian rhythms are skunked. Whatever it might have said on my phone, time is one thing and the body another, and biology being what it is and exhausting emotional roller coasters being what they are, in time each of us is feeling the weight of the day, not to mention the rising heat inside the elevator. Sweat is pooling in my lower back. I grasp my hands over my head and lean right and then left, stretching my waist the way I do in my weekly yoga class. I twist my head from side to side, roll it around, and feel the popping of the small knots with each rotation.

Em starts complaining that her eyes are dry and burning. She says she's thirsty; it feels like she's drying up.

"That's gotta be a metaphor for something," I say. I feel

it too. My eyes are dry, my throat is raw. "Millie, how are you holding up over there?"

"To be honest, not very well." She explains that sitting on this hard, unforgiving floor, her unpadded bones are getting sore and her lower spine feels like it's compressing upon itself, vertebra rubbing against vertebra, the dull ache spreading almost symmetrically around both of her hips.

"Keep up the yoga, Emilia," she says. "Maybe it won't be so bad for you." She stretches out her legs and she twists sideways, hands splayed on the ground for support. Her position reminds me of that famous *Christina's World* painting by Andrew Wyeth, the one with the young woman half prone on the ground, looking up an expansive hill that leads to a house. My mother had a reproduction of the painting hung in the den, hoping it would impart a message of perseverance, I guess—you can get up that hill!—but as a child I was never convinced that the young woman in the painting would be triumphant in her journey. Regardless, it was a beautiful image, rustic and pastoral, so Millie's accidental approximation of the painting ends here. This is hardly a country landscape, this stuffy metal box with the harsh light beating down on us, but Em pulls out of her fetal-shaped funk long enough to notice that Millie is pretzled in this familiar and contorted position. It is uncomfortable to watch an old woman like that, no matter who she is in relation to you, so I shouldn't be as surprised as I am when Em offers to help before I can myself.

"Here, take this," she says, pushing her green backpack across the floor with her foot. "Use it as a pillow."

Millie struggles to even reach it, so Em scoots closer, nudging the bag against Millie's hand.

"That is very nice of you," Millie says, a pained grimace spreading across her face. "I am not sure it will help, though. It looks rather bulky."

"Hang on," Em says, yanking the bag back to unload its contents. Three large textbooks. Physics. Biology. World Cultures.

A thick copy of Tolstoy's *Anna Karenina*. My all-time favorite book.

"You've had *Anna Karenina* in there the whole time?" I flip through a few pages. "Do you know, I had this very copy all through high school and college? I think it's still in a box somewhere. Look," I say, holding up the thick volume to display the pages. More lines are underlined than not, the pages indented by a dark blue ballpoint pen. "Oh, look at my handwriting. It was so much better back then." I look at Em. "Someday you won't need to write by hand so much, and your script will go to shit."

"Are you done?" Millie says from the floor, her voice straining.

"Sorry," I say and put the book down. "Em, what else is in there?"

Em places a thick black spiralbound notebook and a yellow plastic Sony Walkman on top of the textbooks. She pulls off her sweatshirt—revealing a simple gray tank top that does nothing to flatter her scrawny arms or bas-relief clavicle. And yes, there are the stacks of Madonna-style black rubber bracelets circling her bony wrists. She bunches up the sweatshirt, stuffs it into the emptied backpack, and hands the bag back to Millie. Millie takes the bag and is able to shift positions, with her head, at least, resting more comfortably.

While Millie gets adjusted, I turn my attention back to Em's pile of stuff. I grab the Walkman, turning the hard plastic case over and over in my hands. It is waterproof and sturdy and had been my steady companion for most of my high school years, both before and after the crash. "What are you listening to? Is it okay if I open this up?"

"No! Wait!" Em snatches it back, but she is smiling, enjoying the diversion. "Take a guess."

I am more than happy to play at this game. Something, anything to stick a pin in our negative space.

"Oh God. Let me think. 1987, right? I certainly wasn't jiving on Madonna or Cyndi Lauper that year."

"Definitely not." Em laughs. "Think dark."

"Honestly, are we ever able to do anything else?"

"Fair enough."

"Billy Bragg?"

"Darker…"

"The Cure?"

Em shakes her head.

"Talking Heads?"

"Darker…"

"Oh!" I say. "The Smiths, right? It has to be the Smiths! How could I be so stupid? Of course it's the Smiths."

Em holds out the Walkman in a mockingly ceremonial manner and lets me open it. I pull out the plastic cassette tape like it's a big reveal.

"Wow. Look at this." I hold up the cassette tape and examine the archaic specimen as if it has been unearthed from an ancient shrine. The sticker across the top has the words *Smiths Favs* written in a loopy teenage script. "A mixtape. Now there's some ancient history," I say, staring reverently at the rectangle of plastic. I hum a few bars of the band's gloomy song, "There Is a Light That Never Goes Out," and then, because I can never quite carry a tune, I half-sing, half-mumble a couple of lines. Em chimes in, and together we croak out the chorus, an earworm about how it would be a heavenly privilege to die by each other's sides. Depressing, but catchy. It was my favorite song for a long time.

"Oh, can I play it?" I ask, snapping the cassette back into place with a satisfying click, a nostalgically pleasurable sound.

"The battery died before I got on the elevator."

"You sure?"

"Don't you think I would have been listening to it this whole time?"

"Fair enough," I say, cradling the Walkman in my hands, this artifact of my childhood. It is heavier than I remembered. "You know, I vaguely remember their concert. It was just a few months before the accident, right? At GW?"

"Yeah. I was actually thinking about that earlier today. Mom got me and Amy comp tickets, so we went."

"Amy. I wonder whatever happened to her."

"No idea. We stopped talking."

"Right," I say, and that briefly silences us. "I feel bad about that."

"There wasn't anything left to say, you know?" Em says.

I nod. I know.

"She died last year," Millie interjects from the floor. "I saw the obituary."

"What?" Em asks. "Amy?" She looks shocked. She may not be on speaking terms with Amy, but that doesn't mean she doesn't care. She counts on her fingers. "So I guess she would be seventy-six, right? I guess that's not so bad."

"I'd like to think it is," says Millie. "I could use a few more years than that."

"Right. Sorry," says Em, wrinkling up her nose. "How does she die?"

"I am not sure I should tell you, to be honest. But I suppose you'll find out eventually." She pauses. "Car crash."

"That's not funny," Em says.

"I am not trying to be funny. That's what happened."

"So that's our fault too?" Em asks, meaning it as a joke—I think.

"That's not funny either," says Millie. "But no, it's not our fault. Nobody drives anymore. It was a mechanical failure, I'm guessing."

"Wait," I say. "Are you serious?"

"Yes. Cars drive themselves now, Emilia. You'll see."

I am not sure what to do with that tidbit about the future, but it makes enough sense that I don't need to dwell on it. "I mean the mechanical failure. That's a weirdly disturbing coincidence, don't you think?"

"I wouldn't read too much into it," says Millie. "It was never proven to be the cause in our case."

"It was never proven that it wasn't."

"What are you talking about?" Em asks.

I sigh and pull my phone back out of my bag. "I'm sure you've seen this already. I know you have," I say, opening another document and passing my phone back to Em. "Take a look before the battery dies completely."

Em quickly skims the article I have pulled up on the screen—a story from January 16, 1987, about Audi recalling more than five thousand cars because of what it called a "sudden acceleration" defect—and then turns away as if she's been looking at something offensive. "So what? That's not new. And it doesn't change anything," she says. "It says it happens when the car shifts from park. We weren't parked."

"But still, it does open up a question about the reliability of the car, doesn't it? I am not saying that absolves us, but it could have something to do with what happened."

Em snatches the phone from me, her bangs creating a curtain over it as she re-reads the article. "It doesn't change anything," she says. "I was still the one who was driving and Mom's still the one who's dead."

And with that, the light snaps off again. There isn't even a fade to black to ease us into it.

26

Extended Sympathies: Em

October 16, 1986
Brandywine Street, NW
Washington, DC

The funeral was scheduled for a Thursday, a full four days after the crash—enough time for the news to settle in and the
announcement to go out. It was standing room only, a sea of
people dressed in black, many looking more as if they had
come to network rather than mourn, the way they seemed so
determined to be seen shaking hands and to pose for the other
influential guests to take notice. Her mother would have been
proud. But the memory of the service itself is mostly hazy.
Who tossed the dirt? Who eulogized? Em doesn't remember
that either, although she knows it wasn't her. She had barely
spoken since the hospital; there was no way she could have
given a speech.

For her, the memory comes into focus around the food.
After the service, for days on end, there was an unrelenting
delivery of food. Cold cuts and brisket. Salads and cake. Her
family wasn't observant—no need to plan a burial in under
twenty-four hours—but Sam Fletcher's grandfather Saul
Fleishman was, and somehow the message had gotten out. It
was as if the seven days of shiva had been enforced upon them,
a conveyor belt of meals passing through their house. Towers of Tupperware. Distant aunts and uncles were practically
emerging out of the walls, grabbing Em, smothering her into
their voluminous bosoms and sweaty embraces, these people
who were practically strangers.

Friends showed up too. Classmates in ill-fitting dresses and suits, awkwardly offering condolences because their parents had told them it was the right thing to do. That was the worst, seeing her peers. Em didn't want to speak with them, didn't want them looking at her with their pitying eyes.

She withdrew to the Yellow Room, figuring it was too formal for the other kids to feel comfortable enough to go in. She remembers sitting there half-hidden by the heavy silk brocade curtains while balancing a plate of cookies and fruit that had somehow materialized on her lap and thinking about how appalled her mother would be by all of this chaos—how she would have forcefully taken control of it, dictating who should sit where and how the food should be arranged, just to start—when her friend Amy came over and pulled up one of the tightly upholstered antique seats that were normally forbidden to anyone under twenty.

"You have to eat something eventually," Amy said, picking up a small bunch of grapes off Em's plate. "Just try a few."

Em looked at the grapes to avoid looking at Amy.

"Come on, Em," Amy urged. "I mean, there's thin and there's thin. You are starting to look as skinny as those anorexic models in *Seventeen* magazine."

"Isn't that a good thing?" Em muttered.

"Oh my God! She made a joke!" Amy playfully slapped Em's shoulder. "She's back!" Em smiled despite herself. "I saw that," Amy said with a wink.

Em had known Amy since kindergarten. She lived across the street and they went to the same school; there wasn't a thing that Em didn't know about Amy or that Amy didn't know about her. Until the accident. Now even Amy was buying the party line, trying to convince her old pal that it would all be okay, that she didn't do anything wrong.

Amy had come by the moment Em and her dad got back home from the hospital; she had been watching from her kitchen window, waiting for the taxi to pull up to the curb.

"Em!" she cried, grabbing Em in a fierce hug before she had even gotten through the front door. "I'm so sorry!"

Amy was nearly a full head taller, so Em's chin was crushed into her friend's clavicle, bone to bone, when Amy began to cry in deep heaving sobs. It wasn't fully clear who was supposed to be consoling whom.

Em could hardly look at her friend once she pulled free, but she could not miss that Amy's eyes were raw and red and distraught, as if it had been her own mother who had died. The sight of her friend's tears shook her. It was a sign—condemning proof that her best friend was yet another person she had hurt, another person impacted by the loss of her mom, who, after all, Amy had known more than half her life.

But even Amy didn't buy her story. Em's dad had seen to that, cornering the girl in the kitchen when Em withdrew to the bathroom to splash water on her face.

"What are you guys talking about?" Em demanded when she returned to find the two of them deep in conversation.

"Nothing," Amy said, looking to Mr. Fletcher for support.

"Nothing, sweetie," he said, although Em knew that was patently untrue. And later, as they sat on her bed, Em's knees tight to her chest, Amy held tight to the narrative.

"Don't beat yourself up so much," she said. "You didn't do it. I know you feel bad that you were fighting with your mom before it happened, but the accident was so not your fault."

Em's dad clearly had a lock on the story. Em knew that if Amy wouldn't hear her out, nobody would. Amy would go to her grave believing it had been Mr. Fletcher's hand on the wheel.

A few days later, at the shiva, Amy sat there, still being kind, still saying the things people were supposed to say, but rather than feel fortified by her presence, Em was pained by it.

"Do you want some?" She held her plate up to Amy, trying to act as though things between them were going to be okay, but Amy was looking past the top of Em's head.

"I can't believe how many people are here," Amy said.

"Can't you? I'm surprised there aren't more. My mom would have invited even more."

"Yeah," Amy said, plucking a cookie off Em's plate. "Maybe

you're right. And if your mom had planned this, it would probably have been more organized too."

"Riffraff in the morning, VIPs after five. Kids…"

"…in the basement, please," Amy joined in, parroting one of Sally Fletcher's common refrains from their childhood.

"And now look at us," said Em.

"You know, I don't think I've ever even been in this room."

"You haven't."

Amy sniffed. "I can sort of smell your mom in here."

She wasn't wrong. It did smell like an aftertaste of Em's mother's perfume, like a slightly tangy orange. Em deeply wished Amy hadn't pointed that out because she knew she would never be able to un-smell it.

"I read somewhere that we remember things more clearly when there is a strong scent attached to it. Maybe this is like your mom making sure she stays with you," Amy said, probably trying to be helpful somehow, but for Em, that was that. She had nothing left to say to her friend. Em pretended to nibble at a grape, watching as Amy took in the room and all of its stilted formality and hoping that Amy would just fucking leave.

She wouldn't. She just sat there, looking around and commenting on all of the people passing by. "Isn't that guy like a senator or something?" and "That man over there is from the evening news, right?"

Em couldn't care less. At least not until Amy noticed someone who wasn't famous at all.

"Oh my God," Amy said in a giddy whisper, protectively shuffling her chair closer to Em. "He's here. He's walking this way."

Em didn't need to ask who *he* was. She knew. She knew she had to get out of there. She stood up, flipping the plate from her lap and spraying fruit and cookies across the antique oriental rug. She didn't care. She rushed out of the room, through the pantry, and out the back door.

The last thing she wanted was condolences from Christopher Grant.

27

Take Back the Night: Emilia

October 12
9:28 p.m.
Friendship Heights Metro
Washington, DC

As time dribbles on, the darkness slowly lifts and the light inside the elevator becomes gray and flattening—the way it is sometimes when a storm is about to roll in.

"It is possible it wasn't him," Millie is saying, continuing a strain of the conversation we've been having for the better part of an hour. Just the two of us. Em, for her part, has been stewing in the vortex of negativity that is her corner of this space, imploring us to leave her alone, saying she needs to think. The more we press her to try to pick apart our memories with us, the more she withdraws. So Millie and I have taken to rehashing the days and nights surrounding our mother's death without her, hoping that in there, in the shadows of our memories, there might be a clue, something that could both figuratively and quite literally shake us out of our current impasse. Our memories don't always perfectly align, though. And while that is not comforting, the contemplation of it is at least a bit compelling, as if a promise of relief is in there somewhere, even if it is a little painful to excavate.

"It is possible it wasn't him," Millie says again, rubbing the knee of her outstretched right leg. "There's no way to be sure."

I fish a rubber band out of my bag and pull my hair back into a low ponytail. "Of course it was him," I say. "It had to be him. I'm sure of it."

"Who gives a shit?" Em blurts out. Her head is pressed between her knees as if she's been trying to contain her growing exasperation.

"How about that," I say. "The young one finally speaks."

"Fuck you," she snarls, but she's been reeled back into the conversation, like it or not. She can't help herself. She looks up, her face red and blotchy. "What does it matter if he was there or not?"

"It matters," I say, drawing out my words, "because if he came to the shiva it meant that he probably didn't think he had done anything wrong."

"Are you serious? We were all so drunk. He probably doesn't even remember what happened that night at the party at all, never mind what happened between the two of us."

"It's certainly possible," Millie says. "But you would think a person might remember being barfed upon, no?"

It is such awkward phrasing coming from such an elegant-looking lady that Em lets out a small laugh despite herself. This flicker of levity seems to further encourage Millie.

"Just imagine," she says, "if only he'd had to fight off the three of us together that night. Now, that would have been more memorable still."

"Three heads at once?" I say and immediately cringe. "Sorry, that came out wrong. I mean, three heads are better than one. Ugh. That's not so great either."

"It's not a joke," Em snaps.

"Of course it's not," Millie says, admonishing me through narrowed eyes.

"No, you're right, it's not," I say before Em has a chance to retreat. "And in a way, you handled yourself well enough alone. Throwing up on him was, in retrospect, a nice little feat."

"It wasn't a feat," Em says, still snarling. "Maybe you don't remember it clearly, but none of that would have happened at all if I hadn't gotten so drunk in the first place."

"Right," I say, because I know that Em has a long way to go, that Em still thinks that what Christopher Grant did was all her fault, that somehow she had encouraged him to do what he did. It wasn't until later, into the '90s, when I was marching to take back the night and all that, that I finally began placing at least some of the blame for that horrible moment on Christopher Grant himself, where it belonged, whether he remembered it or not.

But it isn't until this very moment that I decide it is time to make sure that blame stays put.

"I need to tell you guys something," I say, gnawing on a cuticle.

"All ears here," says Millie.

Em, however, retreats even further into her ball, her vertebrae sticking out. She looks like an armadillo under attack.

"And?" Millie asks impatiently.

I know what I need to tell them, but I am not sure how to begin. I look around at the scene—the metal walls, the flickering light, my exhausted selves. I decide I need to begin right here.

"Have either of you considered why on earth I would have taken the Metro this morning? I hardly ever take the Metro." Then something else occurs to me. Millie should know. "Hang on. If I was there, then you were there too, right? This morning? My morning. Do you remember what happened?"

"Honey, most days it's a struggle to remember what I had for breakfast."

"You would remember this. You seem to have no problem remembering a lot of other things."

"I'm not sure what to tell you. I honestly have no clear memory of where I was the morning of the thirty-first anniversary of our mother's death, if that's what you mean. I couldn't tell you about the forty-first either. Or the fifty-first. It's all a blur." She bites her lip, thinking. "Wait a second," she says. "How come you didn't go to the Shore today? Isn't that what I did all those years? I only stopped going about ten years ago, when it was no longer possible."

Em briefly lifts up her head. "Why wasn't it possible?"

Why wasn't it possible? I'm curious too.

"At best, the house has become a spawning ground for fish eggs and algae. Most likely, every brick and plank has long since washed out to sea."

I look at her, bug-eyed. Em doesn't need to know about that. It's not relevant to her life. Not yet. Climate change isn't even part of her vocabulary in 1987. Why freak her out even more than she already is? I quickly redirect the conversation.

"You don't remember fighting with Joel this morning?" I ask before Millie has a chance to say anything more about the climate collapse that we are all doomed to have to deal with. That Millie is living through now. "Don't you remember the car breaking down?"

"No," Millie says, "I don't think so. But I remember fighting with Joel a lot around that time—your time—but nothing particular to this day."

"But you remember having the fight about the trees in the front of the house? You've already said as much."

Millie thinks for a moment. "Yes. Of course I remember that." She shakes her head. "And I regret it."

"What do you mean?"

"I should have just let him plant those trees when and where he wanted to. They die, you know, the ones in the sacks. We left them lying there in the front yard for weeks. It was like a standoff, waiting to see who would deal with them first."

"Who caved?"

"Arguably, the marriage caved, dear, that's what matters. And just to be clear, that's not all that collapsed. Sonya blamed it all on me. Everything. Even to this day she sides with Joel, and he died about ten years ago."

I say nothing. I couldn't even if I tried.

"But what about the rest of it?" Em asks, curious enough to move the story along. "What does that have to do with you taking the Metro?"

28

Morning Edition, Part 5: Emilia

October 12, 2017
9:37 a.m.
Brandywine Street, NW
Washington, DC

Clearly—I thought as I climbed into the back of the car and noticed that another passenger was already there—this was going to be that kind of day. I must have hit Uber Pool by mistake. Of course I had. Now it would probably take an extra fifteen minutes to go the mile to Friendship Heights. Not that there was any reason to rush. Not that I had any other place to be.

"Excuse me," I said and squeezed myself in, placing my large red suede purse on the seat between the passenger and myself. I pulled out my phone and began to compose another text to Joel, begging him to call me back.

"Emilia?"

I looked up.

The other passenger was leaning over my bag, staring at me.

A man. Gray hair. Wire-framed glasses. He had a bit of a paunch sticking out from his unbuttoned suit jacket.

"I'm sorry, do I...?"

"Emilia Fletcher, right?" he said, and then it came to me fast. Not all the things I had wanted to say, not the incisive truth-telling or the biting revenge, just the bile that rose up in my throat. Because there he was. He was middle-aged and bloated, but it was definitely him.

"Christopher Grant," the man said, pointing to himself. "From Washington Day School?"

"Yes," I managed to eke out. I felt like I might vomit up my heart.

"How are you? Hey, wasn't that your parents' house where you got in?"

I nodded because I wasn't sure what else to do. Shit. Why couldn't my tongue give shape to any words? Why was it that instead of rage, all that I felt was a suffocating sense of shame? Thirty-one years and it might as well have been a day.

"I'm heading up to check in on my dad," he said, filling the uncomfortable silence. "He's at that nursing home off Military Road. Alzheimer's. Totally sucks. I guess we're that age though, right? Parents getting old, and…" He stopped. What an idiot.

"Right," was all I could say.

"Oh Jesus. I totally forgot."

"It's fine." I tried to focus out the window. Look at the horizon. That's what they tell you to do when you are seasick.

"So how are you otherwise? Married? Kids?"

How the hell was this happening? Was I supposed to make small talk with Christopher Grant?

"Yes," I said despite myself. I tried to keep my focus on the cars in front of us. We were on Connecticut Avenue now, along with what seemed like every other car in DC. "I—"

My phone beeped again, but it wasn't salvation. It was a sheep. I declined the call and shoved it back in the bag. There was no way I could talk to Joel right now.

"Nice ringtone," said Christopher Grant, and I half-smiled in response, mostly in the hopes of shutting him up. No such luck. He just couldn't sit quietly and leave me alone.

"You're looking good," he said.

"Thanks." I could feel my cheeks heating up and it sickened me to realize that his compliment landed, that I actually cared what I looked like to him. And then I heard myself say, because it was polite, "So do you," as if someone else were inhabiting my body. It couldn't be me. Why would I indulge him like that? Thirty years later, no, thirty-one, and he still held the reins.

"Hey," he said. "Do you remember Sandy Wildman?" I shook my head. I did not. "He works in my office now."

I could just feel him begging me to ask for more.

"NRDC," he continued. "Natural Resources Defense Council. Environmental work. Litigation. Trump is keeping us busy with his rollbacks. What an ass. Did you read about the crap he said about the California wildfires yesterday?"

Great. The man who fractured my universe was now trying to save the world.

"So what do you do these days?" he asked. He just couldn't shut up.

"Nothing," I said to the man who had tried to make me give him a blow job more than three decades before, and then I wondered for a moment if maybe I was going insane.

Maybe it wasn't him.

Maybe it had never happened at all.

I forced myself to take a closer look.

He had the same sturdy jaw, the same confident smile. No, I wasn't crazy. It was him; it was the man who had held my head down, the man—no, the boy—who I had vomited all over.

"I heard you went into the TV news biz like your mom," he continued, as if we were at a cocktail party.

I struggled to find something cutting to say, to ask if he remembered what had happened, to demand that he atone for what he had done.

"That was a long time ago," was all that came out. "Excuse me," I said, reaching past him to tap the driver's shoulder. "I can get out here."

"Here?" The driver pointed to the tracking map on the phone propped up on the dashboard. "You go here." He had an indiscernible but probably Eastern European accent. "Just one mile more."

"No. I need to get out now."

"There is traffic…hard to get to side."

"No," I repeated, "this is good. You can let me out here."

"Are you okay?" asked Christopher Grant.

"I just forgot something," I said. "Can you pull over, please?" I asked the driver again, sterner this time, and at the next light he finally did.

"Nice to see you," Christopher Grant called out as I slammed the door shut.

"You too," I said, although *fuck you* was what I meant. Why didn't I just say that? I felt nauseous. Dirty, almost. I wanted to shower. I needed air. I needed space.

There was no way I was getting into another Uber. I would just have to walk the rest of the way to Friendship Heights, and then on the way back I could take the Metro home.

29

Short Circuit: Emilia

October 12
10:23 p.m.
Friendship Heights Metro
Washington, DC

Em unfolds herself and presses her back up against the wall. "So," she says. "You saw Christopher Grant. What of it? I see him all the time. I mean, God, he's in my math class."

"I know. I remember that. But you never speak to him. Never once have you said a word to each other since—"

"And what exactly do you wish *we* would say?" she asks bitterly.

"What she didn't say in the car," Millie says, nodding her head at me.

"Fine!" I jump to my feet. "You're right. I should have said something. I should have spat in his face." I pace. Three steps in one direction, three in another. "But I didn't. I just sat there like a placid fool. Fuck!" I squat down, grabbing my hair into my fists and falling back against the wall.

"It is strange that I don't remember any of that," Millie says almost wistfully. "You would think that running into him like that wouldn't be something I would have forgotten."

"But I don't get it," Em says. "If he doesn't remember anything, then what's the point?"

"Apparently Millie doesn't remember half of it either," I say. There's a bitter taste forming in my mouth. "It doesn't mean it didn't happen. And so what if he doesn't remember anything?

Or maybe he does but he doesn't think he did anything wrong. Which is almost worse. Either way, he should know."

"We were both so drunk," says Em. "So it's not like it was entirely his fault."

"Don't say that," I hiss. "*You* didn't put his hand on your head. *You* didn't push your own head down there. That part of this whole affair was definitely not on us."

Em rolls her eyes. She's no dummy. "And you believe that? That you are so innocent in this?"

"I'm trying to," I concede. "But you know what? Maybe if you are able to see it this way sooner than I did, all of this fucked-up conflicted shit wouldn't be so deeply etched into my brain."

"You do have a point there," Millie says. "Whatever we do or don't remember, Em still has some neuroplasticity up there." She taps her forehead.

"What the hell are you talking about?" Em asks.

"Your brain," Millie says. "Thoughts get entrenched and the longer you believe something, the harder it is to see it any other way. At your age, the brain is still malleable. By my age, the things are quite stuck in the grooves."

"Exactly!" I say. "I can understand *intellectually* that I didn't do anything wrong, but it ends there. But maybe if you can get a handle on that idea sooner, then when you're my age and you run into Christopher Grant, you can hold your head high."

"So now you're blaming me that you felt uncomfortable in that Tuber?"

"You mean Uber?"

"What the fuck. Uber. Whatever. Jesus Christ."

"No, dear," says Millie, granting me a reprieve. "We aren't suggesting that anything is your fault. That's the point. It wasn't our fault. But as much as we understand that, we still feel like it was. Emilia's memories are stuck on a negative track. Your brain is still flexible enough to change that. That could have a very positive ripple effect."

"Is that how you feel about killing Mom too? That it's all *my* fault that you still feel like it's *your* fault?" Em says. I can feel the heat radiating off her cheeks. "Are you going to blame all the shitty decisions you've ever made on me when you can't even agree on your own fucking memories?"

"No, that's not what—" I stammer.

"That's not what we mean," Millie says, finishing my thought. "It's just, look, let's start over. What we are trying to say is that you should be more forgiving of yourself."

"Right, because otherwise, I fuck up your lives."

"No, dear. That's not exactly what—"

"So is this where it starts?" Em cuts in. "That whole business of trying to comfort your earlier self? Because if it is, you're both doing a real shitty job of it."

Millie and I catch each other's eyes. This is indeed where it starts. This is the wedge issue, as it were. All of those years of beating myself up, not just for my mother's death, but for getting drunk in the first place, which was what launched all the dominoes that ultimately toppled me into the driver's seat of my father's car. And I know that for Em, this is in many ways where she feels like it ends, because, not to belabor a point that Millie already made, the trajectory of a life is nothing but a series of decisions and consequences, one after the next, some leading us to better places than others. This we know. The problem is, when we feel overwhelmed the decision-making process itself gets corrupted, and like an overloaded computer, it begins to crash. In Em's case, the window in which we can re-route that circuitry is closing fast.

PART III

30

Morning Edition, Part 6: Em

October 12, 1987
8:41 a.m.
Brandywine Street, NW
Washington, DC

Earlier this morning, after Em stomped down the walkway, grinding the pulp of the noxious ginkgo fruit into the soles of her black Doc Martens, she didn't have much of a plan. It was too early for school, but she couldn't stay in that house. She just couldn't. There was a steady breeze and it was mildly chilly, a situation marginally helped by the fact that Em wore her oversized school sweatshirt. She adjusted her heavy backpack so the fabric didn't bunch up under the straps, and she turned the volume of the Sony Walkman all the way up. It was so loud that a passerby would have heard the bass notes, but for Em the soft foam of the headphones kept Morrissey's voice crooning in and the rest of the world at bay as he imagined how being hit by a bus or a ten-ton truck would be a heavenly way to die, so long as he was by his lover's side.

The lyrics coursed through Em's veins, as if the sulky British singer were serenading her. Almost. Not really, but it was enough for her to enter a different realm for a spell, into a place where she wasn't Emilia Fletcher, daughter of a famous dead woman, and, unbeknownst to all, a matricidal murderess. It allowed her to briefly imagine that maybe someday someone would feel this way about her. Maybe one day she would be deserving of that. She just wasn't sure how she could get to that point. She wasn't sure what could possibly redeem her enough for that door to open, but for that moment she could at least humor herself with the fantasy that maybe someday, somehow, she would be worthy of such love.

Unsure of where to go, and not wanting to decide, Em looked for a sign, for a decision she didn't have to make. It didn't take long. Across the street, a couple of doors down from Amy's house, a shiny red Audi pulled out of the driveway. It startled her. She hadn't realized that their neighbor had that same model car, the one she had been driving when her mother died. Why was it there? Why hadn't she seen it before? It didn't make sense.

Still, it was weird, seeing that car on her street, especially on this day, the first anniversary of her mother's death, so when it turned east toward Connecticut Avenue, she decided to follow it. That made more sense to her than heading to school; it gave her a way to acknowledge the importance of the day when her father would not.

At dinner the night before, when Em's father passed her the carton of chicken lo mein, he sighed deeply and, seemingly out of nowhere, announced that he had decided they should treat the anniversary of the accident like any other day. Maybe in the evening they could share a few memories, he said, but for now Em should go to school and focus on her future.

"That's what your mother would want. She'd want us to simply keep living our lives. Life needs to go on. I think that's the best way we can honor her memory."

"I'm not living much of a life," Em muttered, though her father heard her loud and clear.

"That's up to you, honey. You can make it what you want. But you are Sally Fletcher's daughter, Em. You should embrace that. She was a powerful force, and I know that some of that is in you."

Em took her chopsticks and pushed the noodles around on her plate.

"You wouldn't remember this, Em, but the first anniversary of her own mother's death was the day she asked to be assigned to cover the Nixon campaign. That was her big break. She didn't wallow. She moved on. I think you should too."

"I am not wallowing," Em said testily, though secretly she felt relieved. She had been worried that her father would want to drive out to the country house, which would require passing by the now-repaired metal barrier on the side of the bridge. She was glad not to have to spend the day with him, glad not to have to face the loss of her mother head-on, but all the same, it didn't feel right to do nothing at all.

But what should she do? How could she possibly honor her mother when she felt so responsible for her death? It was too hypocritical.

Of course, there was no keeping up with an Audi, and as soon as it tore past the stop sign and took a right at the corner, Em was on her own. The wind whipped up, blowing her hair around in a manner no amount of Tenax styling gel could ever hold in place. And as if she were being guided by this odd sort of weather vane, she decided she would go whichever way the wind blew her.

After a couple of blocks, the smattering of female ginkgoes gave way to the less olfactorily offensive varieties of trees, some of which were already turning shades of russet and gold, which might have seemed pretty had Em been open to that. As Em walked, the spacious single-family homes of her neighborhood gave way to apartment blocks, and the grand oaks and maples gave way to traffic lights. The red car was nowhere in sight.

Not sure what else to do, she headed south along Connecticut Avenue, past a bleak concrete stretch of the city with a small shopping plaza anchored by a dingy Giant supermarket she'd only been in a couple of times. The first was a few years back when her mother was hosting a small cocktail gathering and Em had hidden herself in the kitchen.

"Em!" her mother had called, pushing open the swinging door just enough to poke her head in. "What are you doing?"

Em was sitting at the breakfast table working on her math sheets and sucking milk up through the green Crazy Straw her

dad had picked up from the drugstore the day before. It made
the milk taste like plastic, but it was fun to watch the liquid
snake up through the tube as she sucked it in with a big slurping
sound.

"Sorry," Em said, assuming her mother had come to com-
plain about her lack of table manners.

"Darling," her mother said, completely missing the drama
being constructed in her daughter's mind. "Would you mind
running to the store? Ruby went home sick and we are almost
out of limes."

Her mother unsnapped her black Chanel purse and entrust-
ed Em with a few dollars. She felt proud handing those crisp
new bills to the cashier, as if the quality of the currency was
somehow a reflection of herself.

This morning, as she passed the Giant, the wind was starting
to pick up, blowing all the leaves and debris toward the west
side of the street. She followed them, turning right on Van
Ness, with the glassy, gleaming new IntelSat building towering
on the corner. It seemed a structure better fitting to Orbit City,
home of *The Jetsons*, the futuristic cartoon Em used to watch
on Saturday mornings, than this quasi-residential area of Washington, DC. It didn't feel as if it belonged and Em wondered if
the space-age-y building would always look as out of place as it
did at that moment. Maybe someday the surrounding neighborhood would grow up to mimic it, with sleek new developments
popping up along the avenue. The city would change, Em knew
that. Life would go on. And isn't that what her dad insisted
her mother would have wanted? The futuristic building was an
omen, neither good nor bad, that one day things would be different in the world. Not for her, though. Em couldn't see how it
could change for her. She was stuck in her head, stuck in time, in
a moment, in a horror she couldn't shake. Her thoughts would
get caught; the deeply entrenched bad memories—the sound,
the cold, the dark surface of the water—formed grooves that
more positive memories couldn't pass through.

The track switched to the song "Frankly, Mr. Shankly." The

melody was upbeat, but the message was bleak and the lyrics ("I'm a sickening wreck") did nothing to help her feel any better at all. She kept spiraling south even as the parade of candy wrappers and discarded potato chip bags started to blow north. All the while Morrissey sang on, his depressive lyrics bouncing around her head. No, she wasn't channeling him. He was channeling her. Why would anyone ever want to die by her side if she should have died a year ago anyway? She should have died a year ago today. This year shouldn't have been hers to have.

Not a week after the accident, once the visitors slowed to a trickle and the pastries grew stale, her father insisted she go back to school. Keep up your routines, he said. It's the only way forward. Not knowing what else to do, she did.

For the first month, Amy was there each morning, waiting on their corner of Brandywine Street with her toothy smile, ready to journey with Em as they always had, but Amy kept up the incessant mantra that Em should stop blaming herself, that she did nothing wrong, and that made the practice of commuting together short-lived. Em stopped trying to convince her friend otherwise and Amy simply gave up. Without a verbal agreement, they each took it upon themselves to walk down different streets or take the city bus. Sometimes they ran into each other along the way, which was awkward, but Em started to leave earlier and earlier so soon even those encounters ceased and Em went to school on her own, where it was even worse. Nobody knew what to say to her and even if they did, she didn't know what to say back. She didn't want their pity. She wanted their blame, but nobody was going to give her that.

One day at the end of English class, several months after the accident, the teacher gently grabbed Em's wrist as the other kids were funneling out for the next period and pulled her back toward the heavy wooden desk at the front of the room.

"Have a seat," Ms. Callahan said, motioning toward the padded leather chair she never sat in herself. That wasn't her pedagogical style.

Em did as she was told, and Ms. Callahan pulled up one

of the metal classroom chairs so that Em was sitting behind the desk in what would normally be considered the position of power. Ms. Callahan sat down opposite.

"Emilia," she said, as a somber look washed over her face. "I read your poem."

Em stared at her teacher. *And?*

"How do I say this?" Ms. Callahan looked at Em as if the girl might give her the answer without her having to ask the question.

"Yes?" Em asked hopefully. Maybe this was finally it. Maybe Ms. Callahan was open to hearing her out when nobody else was.

"I thought, it was…" She paused. "I was going to say that I am very impressed with your use of imagery and the vividness of your imagination. This must have been a very difficult topic for you to write about. But I wanted to tell you that I am giving you an A."

For any other student otherwise averaging Bs and Cs in the class, this would have been welcome news. For Em, it wasn't. She didn't care.

"That said," the teacher continued, filling in the awkward silence Em had left hanging, "it does have me concerned. I wanted to make sure, that, well—" She struggled to articulate her thoughts. "I wanted to make sure that you know I'm here if you ever want to talk to anyone. You know, I lost my mom when I was around your age. I do have an idea of what you are going through."

Again, Em said nothing.

"She had cancer, which is different, I realize. It wasn't sudden like what happened to your mother. But I do know what it's like to lose—"

"I didn't *lose* my mother. I *killed* her."

"Em, it's totally normal that you feel some responsibility, that's fully understandable. It's part of the process of grieving to—"

"This isn't some stage of grief," Em said, cutting her off.

She leaned across the desk and plucked the crisp lined paper from her teacher's hand. "It's the truth."

"Oh, sweetie," Ms. Callahan began, "I know this must all be so confusing—"

"You know nothing," Em said and left the room. She had hoped the heavy oak door would slam shut, but it simply slowed to an unsatisfying click.

ENGLISH 11, Ms. CALLAHAN 2ND PERIOD
Assignment: Write an "I Remember" poem.
Due: December 14
Name: EM FLETCHER

For this week's assignment, write an "I Remember Poem" in
the style of the piece we read by Thomas Hood. Like Hood,
your poem should have 4 stanzas, each with 8 lines. Each stanza
must start with the words "I remember, I remember."

I REMEMBER, I REMEMBER
  A BRIGHT RED COLOR THAT STOOD OUT AGAINST
  THE WET GRAY OF THE LAND,
  THE WARMTH OF THE STEERING WHEEL
  IN THE PALM OF MY HANDS,
  THE SEAT STICKY FROM THE SUMMER HEAT,
  THE SMELL OF LEATHER POLISHED TO SHINE,
  MY HEART BEATING IN SYNC WITH THE DRIZZLING RAIN,
  THE POWER EMANATING FROM THE PEDAL
  UNDERNEATH MY FEET,
  MY MOTHER INSISTING UPON DRIVING FROM THE BACK
  SEAT.

I REMEMBER, I REMEMBER,
  MY FATHER HOLDING TIGHT TO THE STRAP
  SILENT IN THAT WAY OF HIS,
  WHILE MY MOTHER'S SENTIMENT YOU COULD NOT MISS.
  SLOW DOWN, SPEED UP, NO DON'T DO THAT.
  EACH COMMAND FELT LIKE A SLAP,
  I STALLED, SHE SHOUTED, I HIT THE GAS,
  AND THEN THE ENTIRE EARTH COLLAPSED.

I REMEMBER, I REMEMBER
    THE SOUND OF GRAVEL SPINNING OFF THE WHEELS,
    A DEAFENING IMPACT I COULD NOT FEEL,
    THE WATER AS IT RUSHED IN TOO FAST,
    THE SEAT BELT BUCKLE I STRUGGLED TO UNCLASP,
    MY FATHER TUGGED THE STRAP AND I WAS FREE AT
LAST,
    BUT MY MOTHER'S BUCKLE, IT HELD FAST.
    FROM THERE THE PRESS TOLD ALL THE REST.

I REMEMBER, I REMEMBER
    HOW I COULD NOT CRY,
    A BED PILLOW THAT JUST STAYED DRY.
    MY FATHER SAID IT WAS NOT MY FAULT,
    HE SAID HE WAS AT THE WHEEL
    WHEN THE PEDAL GOT CAUGHT.
    I CRIED OUT THE TRUTH WHICH WAS DIFFERENT THAN
THAT,
    BUT EVERYBODY BELIEVED MY FATHER'S LIE.
    ONLY I KNEW THAT IT WAS ME,
    NOT MY MOTHER, WHO DESERVED TO DIE.

31

October 12, 1987
9:47 a.m.
Wisconsin Ave
Washington, DC

Back on the street, the winds had changed and Em let them push her. She headed north up Wisconsin Avenue, passing the Sears department store with the art deco facade—a store her mother used to refuse to go into. She had spent time there with her dad though, in the automotive department, poking around, back when tinkering was his thing. But that was years ago. It had been a long while since he had tried to engage her in his hobbies, and longer still since she had gone shopping with her mom.

Em had been walking for more than an hour. In the distance, she could see Fort Reno, a Civil War defense post at the highest point in the city—less a tourist destination than a small hill with myriad radio and satellite towers stretching up like stalagmites, some of which were connected to the very television station where her mother had made her name. She passed that too, the Washington bureau of WBS News.

When she was little, Em's mother used to let her sit in the anchor chair or watch the broadcast from the control room, and she remembers feeling very important, the way all of the adults there treated her with what felt like deference and respect.

The last time she had been there, she was twelve. School was off—it was professional development day or something like that. Take Your Daughter to Work Day didn't exist back then, but her mother told her it was important that she know a thing or two about the real world. That morning she had Em put on a simple blue shift dress and told the show's director to put her daughter to work. Em ran around offering coffee to guests in the greenroom and even ferrying videotape to and from an edit bay to the control room when a segment was changed. The director—her mother told her to call him Mr. Johnson, but everyone else called him Doc—said Em was a big help, and, after everything wrapped, he even let her read from the teleprompter.

"3, 2…you got this, kid…1!" Mr. Johnson's cheerful voice carried into Em's earpiece, but just as the words on the screen started to scroll the curly cord fell down the side of her face and her mother, watching from behind the camera, motioned frantically for Em to push it back in place.

Em tried to focus on the teleprompter instead. Wasn't that what they said, that the show must go on? Just read the words, how hard could this be? But she couldn't get the words out.

"Cut!" Mr. Johnson bellowed. He walked out from the control room and went over to Em, leaning over the anchor desk and whispering as if what he had to say was a state secret: "You can do this. I know you can. It's in your blood."

Em glanced over at her mom, but her mother appeared to be deep in a conversation with one of the crew.

"Look," Mr. Johnson said in a kindly conspiratorial fashion. "Just imagine that everyone in here is naked. Then they are the ones who should be nervous, eh?" He had a vague accent that sounded British but was in fact squarely Canadian. Either way, there was something about him that put her at ease.

"Naked?" she asked.

"As the day they were born."

Em blushed. "But that would be weird, don't you think?"

Mr. Johnson gave her a reassuring smile that formed a bracket of wrinkles around his mouth. This was a man who smiled a lot. "You can do this, Em."

And she did. He cued her and she did it. Simple as that.

"Hello, America! Today is a brand new day!" she began, parroting her mother's catchphrase. "It's Friday, June 15, 1984. It's a beautiful day here in the nation's capital and do we have a show for you. Kathy Klark will be cooking up some complicated-looking confections that are so simple you can bake them with your kid... Speaker of the House Tip O'Neill will be on the hot seat for my Washington Weekly Wrap...and movie star Sigourney Weaver is here to bring us in on a little secret about busting ghosts... But first, the news."

Afterward, back in the control room, Mr. Johnson patted Em on the back and said she was a natural. Her mother told her that she needed to sit up straighter and smile more. Her mother may have also said other things, nicer things, but that's all Em remembered, part of the gauntlet of memories that seemed fitting for this particular day.

It was also fitting that today, just a handful of years later, on this seemingly aimless journey, as soon as Em was just half a block north of the bureau, just as she was thinking about that studio tour, the batteries of her Sony Walkman began to die. It sounded like Morrissey was slurring his words—and then the song cut off entirely.

She stopped at the edge of a small triangular park—it was more a traffic median than anything else, barely stretching the length of a city block. She rested her heavy backpack on a wooden bench so she could stuff the dead Walkman inside.

"Em?"

Startled, Em spun around.

A man wearing a rumpled white shirt and a dark blue tie sat one bench over. He held a ceramic coffee mug emblazoned with the network call letters *WBS News*. He held up the mug and smiled. Em recognized him immediately.

"Oh, hello, Mr. Johnson," she said, minding her manners as her mother would have wanted.

"Doc," he corrected.

Em nodded, unsure of how else to respond.

"What brings you here?"

What should she say? Today is the anniversary of my mother's death and I am feeling lost and adrift? That seemed a bit much.

"The batteries died," she said, quickly pulling the yellow plastic Walkman out of her bag as evidence.

He smiled knowingly. "What were you listening to, eh?"

She told him and he smiled again.

"Oh yes. The Smiths. Do you know we almost had them on the show?"

That caught her attention. Elton John, Kenny Loggins, even Tina Turner had appeared on the show. But the Smiths?

"Really? When?" She pushed the bag aside and sat down on the edge of the bench.

"Last summer. They were in town for a concert."

"Right," Em said. She had gone with Amy, when they were still friends. "I was there. They wanted the Smiths to go on *Sunrise America*?"

"It wasn't a very serious plan. As soon as Chuck—you know, the executive producer of the show, I'm sure you've met—as soon as he heard a few tracks, he laughed the producer who pitched the idea out of the room," Doc said, grinning at his own recollection. "She thought it might help Sally connect with a younger audience, but Chuck disagreed."

The mention of her mother's name triggered an awkward pause, but Em quickly shook it off. "I guess the Smiths aren't exactly the right tone for a morning show."

"That's what the EP said. But they're good, right? You like them? I haven't heard much. I'm more of a classic rock man myself."

"I'd let you listen, but…the batteries."

"Of course," he said with another broad smile. This time Em smiled back, enjoying this interaction in spite of herself.

"Why aren't you at work?" she asked.

"The show just ended. I needed a little break. But the real question is, why aren't you at school?"

"It hasn't started yet."

He looked at his watch. It was almost eleven o'clock. "Your school must start late."

"Yeah. I mean, I didn't want to go."

"You don't like school?"

"No. It's okay. I just didn't want to go today, you know?" She looked down at the patchy grass. "It was a year ago today…" She trailed off.

Doc closed his eyes for a moment. "Yes. That's right. I am so sorry."

"Don't be."

"What do you mean? It's terrible what happened."

"No, I mean, why do people say that? Everyone tells me how sorry they are. It's stupid, you know? Like, what does that mean? Sorry for what? Sorry that they weren't there to stop me? Sorry they didn't somehow keep us from getting into the car? It's just stupid."

"You do know it wasn't anybody's fault, don't you?" Doc said very gently.

"Sure, whatever."

"There was a mechanical failure."

"That wasn't proven." Em kicked at the dirt.

"Audi recalled all of those cars. It was a pretty big story."

Em was silent. That didn't matter to her.

"I see. Well, whatever happened, Em, your mother's death was most certainly not your fault."

"Yes, it was!" she said, aggressive and exhausted. "I was the one who lost control."

They sat in silence for a few beats after that.

"Do you mind if I join you on that bench?" Doc finally asked.

"Whatever," Em said and pushed her backpack over to make room.

"You're carrying a heavy load there," Doc said as he settled into place.

"Textbooks," Em muttered. "And a can of Diet Coke."

"No, no. Not what's in your bag. What's in your head. That's a lot to carry around. You must miss her a lot."

"Miss her? I just told you I killed her."

"Right." He shut his eyes, as if trying to call up a memory. "I don't see matricide being part of this story, to be honest. But I am not here to judge. You feel like you did it, that you are responsible, then that's what you feel. That's your truth to bear. A heavy load, indeed. I'm sure I wouldn't be the first if I tried to convince you it wasn't your sin to atone for?"

Em did not feel the question even warranted a response.

"Okay…" He thought for a moment.

Em could feel a lump building in her throat. "What should I do?" she blurted out, suppressing a tear.

"What do you mean? Why do you need to do anything at all?"

"What? I should just live with myself, just accept that I'm responsible for my own mother's death and that's it?"

Doc thought a moment. "It seems to me that you might feel better if you could do penance? I'm guessing you aren't Catholic. A few Hail Marys won't do?"

"Hardly."

"Then I do see how this is a tricky situation for you. You want to make it up to your mom. You want to serve out a punishment for what you feel that you did."

"What I did do."

"Of course. Forgive me. So. The question is, what is it that you need? If nobody believes you, nobody can forgive you, and you are having quite a bit of trouble forgiving yourself. So how do you move on?"

That was of course the rotting heart of the matter. It was why she was stuck; it was why she couldn't decide which way to turn; and it was the reason that after the funeral and after life kicked back into gear, Em had swallowed a fistful of aspirin. After that, she was required to see a psychotherapist two times a week.

At the therapist's office, he would ask her if she thought about hurting herself. Em would stare out the window to avoid answering that question. The suite was on the tenth floor of a building on Wisconsin Avenue with large windows tinted gray by a layer of grime. From the beige tweed sofa, she could see over the rooftops and on a clear day she could even make out houses in Chevy Chase. She often tried to pick out which one might belong to Christopher Grant, a little game she would play with herself, which mostly made her feel worse, but in a good way, like picking a scab.

"What is it that you see out there?" the therapist finally asked during one session.

Em turned to look at him, a middle-aged man in a tweed jacket that matched his furniture pulled tightly over his paunch, his legs crossed, a yellow notepad balanced on one knee. Em squinted to make out the scribble, but the paper seemed mostly blank.

The therapist smiled kindly and pushed his glasses up the bridge of his nose, eager to hear what she had to say. Overly eager. She felt sorry for him. It wasn't his fault she was such a bad patient, but in fairness he never seemed to listen to what she had to say. Well, he listened, but he didn't *hear* her. She had tried at first, she really had. She confessed all her sins, but he made it apparent that he perceived her admission of guilt as Freudian, not factual, that it was normal for someone in mourning to feel as she did, that the loss of a mother would logically warrant an even deeper (and often more distorted) mourning than most. In the fog of grief, he would remind her, it could be difficult to see clearly.

"Em?" the therapist pressed, jutting his chin in the direction of the window. "What's out there?"

"Part of the reason I'm here, I guess."

"What do you mean by that?"

Em could feel how pleased he was that she had finally strung together a partially complete sentence, but that didn't make her want to say any more.

The sessions continued for the better part of the year, but as for revelatory breakthroughs, that was as good as it got. The therapist took off for the month of August, and after that Em never returned. Short of mumbling answers to her teacher when called on in class, her father remained the only person she actually spoke to, and with him it was just one ongoing fight.

But now she was talking to Doc. He wasn't actually a doctor, but he was doing something that the therapist couldn't. He was getting Em to speak.

"I don't know, I feel like I'm going crazy. Imagine how it would feel if nobody believed you, like what if you accidentally killed your wife but nobody thinks it is at all your fault."

"For starters, you just said it was an accident. So there's that. Also, I don't have a wife. But let me ask you something. What if you're right? Forget what your father said, what everyone thinks, eh? Forget mechanical issues. What if it is your fault, as you insist? What can you do about it from this point forward? You can't bring your mother back, that's a given. But can't you let her live on through you a little? You are her legacy, like it or not. I realize I only knew your mom professionally, but from what I knew of Sally, it seems to me she'd want you to make the best of that."

Em shook her head. "No. I don't think that's what she would want." It wasn't much in the way of words, but it was more than she had given to the therapist. The rest Em couldn't bring herself to say out loud. She couldn't say that if she was never the person her mother wanted her to be when her mother was alive, how could she be so now?

"I should probably go," she said, standing up and heaving the bag back over her shoulders.

"Hang on," Doc said. He pulled out his wallet. "Let me give you my card. If you ever want to talk, I'm around. And if you ever want an internship, we'd be honored to have you."

Em took the card and shoved it in the back pocket of her jeans.

"Thank you for listening," she said. He wasn't wrong. Not entirely. Something did have to change.

She continued north, passing more markers that brought snapshots of the past, looking for signs that would tell her what direction to go. Rodman's Market, where she and Amy used to run in for a quick snack between classes. The Chevy Chase Ballroom, where her mom took her to ballet class every Saturday until she was around ten and was told her feet were too flat for pointe.

A bus zipped by too close to the curb. She took a step back, causing her to briefly lose her balance and break the trance.

A full year had passed and not a day had gone by when she didn't feel a sudden swirling of nausea or increase in her pulse. How long would this last? It was too much. Everything little or big had the potential to set her off. A red car zipping by. Pancakes. That mother pushing her toddler in a stroller, blocking her path. That one was obvious. That was the definitive sign. The moment she saw them, she knew she had to cross to the other side of the street, which landed her in front of the Jenifer Street entrance to the Friendship Heights Metro.

The elevator entrance. She figured that was a sign, too, a message for her to descend. Really descend. Maybe that was the answer. If she couldn't decide how to move her life forward, maybe the trains could decide her fate for her. It was such a relief, this thought, this idea that she could just hand her pain over to some external force. Yes, she decided, the trains would tell her what to do. Whichever comes first.

Southbound, she steps aside.

Northbound, she jumps Anna Karenina style onto the tracks.

32

Unhappy Families: Emilia

October 12
10:49 p.m.
Friendship Heights Metro
Washington, DC

Time keeps ticking forward, but I am exhausted and the light has stayed stubbornly on for more than an hour, making sleep difficult if not impossible.

Mostly to fill that time, but also because I am tired of trying to think of what to say to Millie or putting up with Em's funk, I have taken to reading passages from *Anna Karenina* out loud. I start, of course, at the beginning, with Tolstoy's famous maxim—"*All happy families are alike; each unhappy family is unhappy in its own way*, yada yada"—but partly because things are getting tedious (it isn't easy sitting with oneself for hours on end, even if there are three of you), partly out of a nod to an aspirational thought that somehow this could all end soon, and partly because I've read the book more times than I can recall—I skip forward, only reading the enthusiastically annotated and underlined passages.

"Oh, this was a good one," I say and recite one of Anna's interior monologues, which has been so deeply drenched in yellow highlighting ink that the color seeps through the page. "*'No, you're going in vain,' she mentally addressed a company in a coach-and-four who were evidently going out of town for some merriment. 'And the dog you're taking with you won't help you. You won't get away from yourselves.'*"

"Well, well," Millie says from her corner, her old bones

cushioned by a variety of our bags donated to the cause. "'You won't get away from yourselves,'" she parrots the phrase. "Isn't that fitting?"

"Like a glove," I concede with a dramatic sigh. There's a dog-eared page toward the end, so I turn to that.

"Oh, look, you're at the pivotal part," I say. "Yup, right where she jumps under the train." I hold the book out at arm's length so I can focus better on the text. "'...*and at that instant she was terror-stricken at what she was doing. 'Where am I? What am I doing? What for?' She tried to get up, to throw herself back; but something huge and merciless struck her on the head and dragged her down on her back...*'"

I put the book down in my lap and turn to look at my younger self. Em is still sitting with her knees tucked into her chest. Her pale, bird-like arms are wrapped around her legs as if she herself were a package. She's no longer fixated on the floor at least, and I am able to look directly into her bloodshot eyes, and Em, in turn, is able to look back.

"What?"

"You don't do it, you know?" I say.

She drops her gaze again to the red linoleum floor. "Don't do what?" she mutters, although she knows. Of course she does. True, it hasn't been in the front of her mind for much of the day—there have been some distractions, after all—but Em has not forgotten her original intention to play Russian roulette with her life. I sure as heck haven't. I've been thinking about it quite a bit. I've known for hours that this particular elephant in the room—one of many elephants, to be sure—needed to be addressed. I know full well why Em got into the elevator this morning. Millie must know this too. After all, it's not easy to forget a suicide attempt. I've tried to push it out of my mind. I'm sure Millie has too. But here I am, bringing it to the fore.

"You don't jump," I say again. "You chickened out that morning. I mean this morning. Anyway, assuming you ever get off this elevator, the northbound train comes first, but you won't do it. You won't jump."

After a pregnant pause, Em asks, "How do you know that?"

"What do you mean, how do I know? Millie and I are here, aren't we? We wouldn't be if you had succeeded."

Em thinks this over. "Maybe it's like a threat. If I don't jump, you're what I will become. You're like the ghosts of my future, middle-aged and old. Like some kind of cautionary tale. Maybe when this nightmare is over and I get to the Metro platform, I'll be inspired to finish the job."

"A cautionary tale?" Millie pipes in from her corner. She places her hand over her heart, feigning dismay. "That's not a nice thing to say."

"To be honest, it's not like either of you seem like very happy people. Why would I want to go through all of this just to get to that?"

Sonya is the first word that comes to mind. "Are you kidding me? I don't have to justify my life to you. If anything, it should be the other way around."

"Right. Like I'm supposed to somehow reengineer my brain and—"

"That's not what we said."

"Yes, it is." Em digs in. "And if you want to inspire me, you have to explain to me why it's worth my while to keep going at all."

"That's ridic—" I start, but Millie quickly interrupts.

"Hang on," she says. "It is a fair enough point, now that Em mentions it."

"So you're saying I have to justify my existence, as if I'm on trial?" I snap at Millie.

"Perhaps."

"It couldn't hurt?" Em says with an apologetic shrug of her bony shoulders.

"Wait. Why me? Wouldn't it make more sense if you ask her?" I point at Millie. "If you want a carrot to keep you going, you may as well go for one closer to the finish line. Millie, what roses are you smelling after all these years?"

"Oh, that's precious," Millie says, sitting up. "But you know,

Emilia, there actually are some roses in that thornbush you like to get stuck in. I know you know that. You could just do a better job focusing on them. If you don't, it's not good. Not just for you. For me too."

"So now I'm the one who's getting advice? I thought we were trying to help Em here?"

Millie looks at herself—at me—at forty-seven. It's all flashing back. "Things could change. There's room for improvement for both of you."

"But not for you?" I ask, somewhat hopeful. Because, honestly, if Millie has her act together—if by the time I'm seventy-seven things are in fact coming up roses—fine, yes, that is something I would like to hear.

"I didn't say that, dear," Millie says.

"You aren't making a great case, you know," Em interjects. "I'll get to seventy and then—"

"Seventy-seven," Millie corrects her.

"Whatever. I'll be old. If I keep going, if I don't jump, I'll just wind up old and filled with regret that I try to smooth over with some botulism injections?"

"No, that's not it," I say, jumping in before Millie has a chance to respond. "She's still lobbying for us to make course corrections. So you, I, don't have to become her."

"But that makes no sense. We've already talked about this. If I change anything from this point on, won't that change what happens to you too? Isn't that what we said before? And then you might not even have come to the Friendship Heights Metro. Our life would be set on a different course. We discussed this. It's science fiction 101."

"Yes, Em. I read *A Wrinkle in Time* too," I say. "But the truth is that none of us knows if what happens in here will impact anything beyond these walls. There's no way to know."

"It's not like this is a black hole," says Em. "All actions have reactions. Something would have to change. I've been thinking about it. You can look it up in that physics book over there."

She nods toward the stack of textbooks she's pushed into the unoccupied corner.

Millie laughs dryly.

"What?" Em and I ask.

"Well," says Millie. "It's just that from where I'm sitting, that textbook is sixty years old. A lot has changed."

"So everything I've learned from it is irrelevant?"

"No, no. That's not what—" Millie starts to say, but then she just stops. She takes a deep look at Em, then at me. Her eyes are raw and red and probably as dried up as mine feel. "May I see that?" she asks, pointing to the textbook.

"Physics?"

"Yes. That one."

"Why?" Em asks.

"I'm not sure. Maybe it will jog a memory."

Em pulls herself up to get the textbook and hands it to Millie. She stands over her like she is expecting Millie to open it, maybe look up some now disproven fact, but that is not what Millie does. She simply holds it up close to her face, inhales deeply, and then gives it back.

"Thank you, dear."

Em takes it back, confused.

"What was that?" I ask.

Millie smiles knowingly. "Smell it. You'll see."

So Em hands the book to me, and I do as I am told. "I don't get it."

"The smell," Millie says. "Doesn't it connect you right back?"

"I guess it smells like homework," I say, and we laugh.

"Exactly," says Millie. "Not something I ever thought I would smell again."

"Have you wanted to?" asks Em.

Millie thinks for a moment. "No. Not that. The opposite is more like it."

"Meaning what?"

Millie looks at me as if I might understand what she's getting at. "Meaning I've long tried not to think about it at all. My youth, that time in my life."

It's true. Yes, there is the annual trip to the Eastern Shore, the deification of my mother, that sort of thing, but if I ever find my mind taking me back, really trying to remember how it felt to be my seventeen-year-old self, I just shut it off. But isn't that mindfulness? I see the thought, I acknowledge it, and I ask it to move along, thank you very much.

"It's impossible, though," Millie continues. "I smell this textbook and it reminds me of being you. And that hurts."

"If this is your attempt at convincing me that my life is worth living…"

"No. Sorry, dear. It's just that when I have thought of you over the years, even if I try not to think about you, sometimes I want to yell at you or slap you. But I've also thought that if I could, I would just want to hug you, like that could make it all better somehow. Of course, I know it won't. It won't change a thing." She folds her hands in her lap and looks down at them as if the bulging knuckles and pulsing veins could offer her wisdom somehow. She sighs and looks up at Em. "But maybe we should give it a try?"

"Ugh!" Em mutters.

I try to contain my grin. "Millie, I don't think your youngest self is quite ready to hug you either."

"It's just…weird," Em says. "And…"

"And?" I ask.

Em bites her lips, working something out. "Like, maybe she wants to hug me, you know? But when I look at her…and you…it's just…I can't exactly explain. I just can't."

She's right. Now that I think of it, in all of this time together, we haven't touched each other at all.

"What do you think would happen if we did?" Millie asks.

Em sighs. "Do you remember anything from that book?" she says like she is trying to change the subject.

"Is there a chapter on time travel?" I say, changing it back.

"No. I'm serious."

"Not really. I remember the smell, but my memory of physics pretty much ends before you open the cover."

"Can you hand it to me?" Em asks. I toss the book at her, with very bad aim and maybe a little too much force. It hits the wall and ricochets halfway back to me.

"I guess I'm still struggling with physics," I say.

"I'm doing fine in that class," Em says, reaching for the book.

"It was a joke."

"Not funny." She turns a few pages. "Here. You have to remember this." She splays the book open and pushes it back in my direction, spinning it around so the words are easy to read.

I read the chapter heading. *Newton's Law of Motion.* "Actions have reactions. What of it? You think if we hug each other, something will change?"

"No, no. Well, maybe. But it's not that. It's just... Wait!" She points at the page. "This is it."

"What?"

"This!" Em jumps up and begins to pace. "Her forehead. Maybe that's why she had those bruises. It has to be that."

"I'm not sure I understand," Millie says.

"That autopsy report. That's what it said."

"There are a number of things that could explain those injuries, dear."

"No. This makes sense. She was leaning forward between the front seats, and when the car hit the railing, her head must have hit something. Like the dashboard, or, I don't know. Something. But the force threw her forward. That must be what happened."

"But she wasn't next to me when I crawled out," I say. "She wasn't up front."

"And what about the seat belt?" Millie suggests.

"Maybe it was loose. But it's what kept her from going through the windshield and pulled her back or something," Em says slowly, mulling things over. "That might help explain the jam. Yeah, like, if her seat belt was on, it could have extended that way they do when you lean forward."

"Meaning what?" Millie and I both ask.

Em looks at us, her big bloodshot eyes looking at once both incredibly sad and humbly proud, like she's just completed a difficult puzzle.

"It's just, I don't know for sure, but I just had this weird murky memory of her pushing me aside. And reaching past me. Right before we spun out and crashed over the rail. But it doesn't seem possible. Why would she do that, right? It doesn't make sense. But that bruise on her forehead. I don't know how else to explain that. I can't prove it, but I guess there is a part of me that wonders if it explains it."

"Explains what?"

"You don't get it? This is what I was trying to say before. It wasn't a mechanical failure, right? It's just...maybe Mom tried to take control of the car."

Millie and I look at each other. We both remember a lot of things about what happened in those moments, but our mother grabbing the steering wheel is not one of them.

33

SPEAK MEMORY: EM

There is a split second of memory endlessly floating in and out of Em's mind. It feels like a gaseous substance, impossible to grasp. She knows that if it's real, her mother's death means one thing. If it's not, if it this is just a figment of her distorted imagination, then that would be another thing entirely. Em knows this. She also knows that in her brain—unlike Emilia's and definitely unlike Millie's—her memories are fresh. But does that fact make them any more real?

She remembers the wet road, the road signs flying past. The sound of her mother's voice is still so clear it feels like she is next to her. Em remembers wanting to turn around and tell her mother to shut up. She wanted to tell her to put down her hand and sit back in her seat, that she was making things worse. She remembers that sweet cloud of perfume wafting off her mother's wrist that made Em want to gag. Who wore perfume when they were spending a weekend on the Shore? She remembers thinking that. She remembers swatting at her mother's arm, begging her to please stop, to please just let her concentrate on the road. But her mother didn't stop, so Em couldn't help herself. She turned around, without slowing down. The car swerved and then her mother pushed past her. And now, Em remembers something new. Her mother called her an idiot and grabbed for the wheel.

Is that what happened? Was that the last thing her mother ever said to her? If so, that would be best to forget. Of course she forgot. Who wants to remember that? But did she really try to get control of the car? Was that true? Her father insists it was him, that he was the one who grabbed the wheel. By the time they emerged from the water, he was telling anyone who would listen that he was the one driving the car all along. But pushing aside that obviously falsified narrative—this part Em remembers clearly, how he had been leaning the other way the whole drive, holding on to the strap over the passenger side door like he was holding on for dear life, doing everything he could to stay out of this mother-daughter drama—there is something that hasn't made any sense.

It wasn't him who drove the car over the bridge. To her, there is no question about that. But Em has no memory of herself making a hard spin of the wheel just before they crashed over the barrier.

People don't always remember things clearly; Emilia and Millie are certainly proof of that. So maybe, depending on the truth of this sliver of memory now coming to light, an inconvenient memory that has been either suppressed or erased over the past year, maybe she didn't do it.

Maybe Sally Fletcher—the beloved, ebullient, always-in-control Sally Fletcher—maybe in a way she actually killed herself.

34

October 12
11:16 p.m.
Friendship Heights Metro
Washington, DC

The light in the elevator is gentler now, dim, but it is enough to be able to see each other. The buzzing of the fluorescent bulbs has either stopped or I have gotten so used to it that it barely registers. It is probably the dark of night outside. Metro service will be suspended soon. Even on Wisconsin Avenue, the traffic would be slowed to a trickle, a smattering of black town cars shuttling home lawyers and lobbyists who worked too late as well as taxis and Ubers transporting those who got too drunk at a bar.

Normally I would be asleep by now, yet here we sit. Me, myself, and I, wide awake and staring at each other, unsure of what to say.

"So?" Em presses. "What do you think?"

"I just…that's just not how I remember it," I say.

"Me either," Millie agrees.

"Exactly!" Em's voice is rising. "You don't remember. You also don't remember riding in that, whatever you call it, Tuber—"

"You mean Uber," I say.

"Whatever, riding in a fucking car with him. Maybe your memories got all fucked up by all the birthing and botulism and, I don't know, just all the crap you've ever done over the course of this whole fucking life of ours."

"And?" I say.

"I don't know. Maybe all these years that you—me, whatever—we just suppressed it. Like, we just locked it away?"

The truth is, while I don't know if Em is right, I don't know that she is wrong. Maybe it did happen that way. And if so, maybe it does change things somewhat. Before we can debate it, the elevator shakes.

"What the...?" I grab the handrail, preparing for I don't even know what.

The light flickers.

There is a quick flash.

"Did you see that?" Em asks, pointing at the door.

Millie and I look up.

My heart is racing. I can't believe it.

There is a tiny gap between the doors. It's no wider than my pinkie, but it's there. An opening.

Em and I both jump up, quickly digging our fingertips into the gap and pulling on the steel frame as hard as we can. It works. The space widens. Just a little, before our fingers slip against the smooth steel. We jerk them back before they get smashed.

The doors slam shut, then bounce open just a touch, revealing a small sliver of space.

"Wait..." Em says. But we know. We are all thinking the same thing. We are not done. We are not giving up. We will try again, and this time we will wedge something in. "We need something slim to start," she continues, energized by the idea.

"Like what?" I ask. "There's not much here."

"Maybe that phone thing of yours? It's not that thick, but it seems sturdy."

"My phone? Are you kidding? It could fall down the shaft. Or crack. And then we'd have lost the last glimmer of hope of possibly reaching someone."

"I don't know how those things work, but it doesn't seem that thing is doing a great job of that."

I have to remind myself not to snap back at her. I'm the

adult here, after all. Or one of the adults, anyway. "There might still be a small charge," I say. "And if the winds shift outside, the cell reception could get stronger. You never know. Also, it has the flashlight, which, if that fails on us completely"—I point at the fixture radiating light from the ceiling—"could prove to be of some use."

"She's right," Millie agrees. "The phone could still come in handy."

Em flashes a petulant glance at both of us. "So then what?"

I hold up the nail file. "This?"

"That's like a millimeter thick," says Em. "Save it for later. In case your manicure gets messed up."

I look at the blood-red polish coating my nails. I just had them done the weekend before, a monthly mother-daughter date Sonya and I have at the salon. Sonya usually gets cute little daisy decals on top of mint green or unicorns on silver. This time she got emoji decals, including a laugh/cry emoji, a couple of hearts, and a poop. My choice was always more convention-al—a single color, usually this one.

"Are you trying to be funny right now?"

"I don't know," Em says. "Are you?"

Millie sighs. "Would you please stop bickering? Both of you." She reaches into her purse and pulls out a pen. "Just try this."

Em shrugs. "I guess it's worth a shot." She plucks the pen from Millie's grasp, holding it up and examining it like it is something precious. "You need to shove it in there super fast while Emilia and I pry the doors apart," she says and then hands it back to Millie.

Millie and I share a look that borders on pride. Look at that girl, confident, taking command.

Em and I return to the prying and pulling, our fingertips white from the strain.

"Now!" shouts Em, when the opening widens just enough, and Millie shoves the ballpoint pen between the two doors.

"There," she says, deeply inhaling the thin stream of cool

air flowing in.

There, indeed. Miraculously, it holds without being crushed and there is now a quarter-inch-wide crack between the doors.

We all stand back, admiring how it protrudes from between the metal doors as if it were yet another sword in a stone.

"And now?" I ask.

"Now something bigger," Em says, reaching for the thick biology textbook that had been pushed to a corner.

"Too big," says Millie.

"There's no way," I say.

"Let's just try, okay?" Em says and hands the heavy tome over to Millie.

Head shaking, I join Em in prying apart the doors again as Millie attempts to work the spine into the tiny space.

Of course it doesn't work. As soon as Em and Millie pull the doors wide enough, the pen falls out and they fling their hands back so they don't get crushed as the doors slam back together.

Luckily, Millie has another pen in her bag. She holds it up like a conductor, and we know what to do. Soon, a pen is back in its critical place, secured to the floor by Millie's foot, and we are trying to think through what next to wedge in that crack.

Which is how, in fairly short order, we sacrifice house keys, Mille's eyeglass frames, even some shoes. One of my kitten-heeled booties is the first piece of footwear to hold the doors, followed by the toe of Millie's sturdy pumps. Every item we can think of is forced into the crack one by one until finally the textbook is able to fit after all, and not just the spine.

"We did it!" Em squeals. She pulls her hands away and the book holds steady. The full ten-plus inches of its length is keeping the doors apart on top of the scaffolding of pens, clothing, and shoes.

"And now?" I ask again, sitting down on the opposite side of the elevator to better admire our work.

"Now we look," says Em, and she sticks her head through the crack in that way one might when they are just seventeen years old and don't yet have enough executive functioning to think through the fact that if the doors were to suddenly shut, she would be instantly decapitated.

Millie, wiser, grabs the waistband of Em's jeans and throws her to the floor next to me, surprising both me and Em with the sudden show of septuagenarian force.

"No," she says, standing tall and mildly triumphant over the two of us, if not a little surprised herself. She places her hands on her hips, superhero style. "If anyone is going to risk getting guillotined, let it be me. I have a lot less to lose."

35

JUST THE THREE OF US: EMILIA

Millie braces herself between the two doors and Em and I crouch down, each grasping one of Millie's ankles to anchor her so she doesn't fall out as she cranes her neck into the blackness.

"Hello?" Millie calls, and her greeting ricochets back. *Hello? Hello?*

Millie calls out again.

The three of us are silent and still and desperate for a reply but nothing comes other than echoes.

Millie pulls herself back into the box. "So now what?" she asks, wiping her hands on her rumpled skirt.

"We jump, I guess?" Em suggests, wincing as she hears herself say it.

"No!" I grab Em's wrist. "We most certainly do not just jump."

Em looks at my hand touching her. Millie puts her hand on top. I can feel them. They can feel me. It's a weirdly kumbaya moment but also completely awkward, like when you're a kid sitting in an assembly and your leg accidentally but not brushes against the person you have a crush on.

Still, it is happening. And it is okay.

"Fine, I won't jump," Em says, gently shaking us off. "But then what?"

"Hang on." I hold her wrist even tighter. "We need to think this through."

"There aren't that many options," she says. "It's a black void out there."

"Exactly," I say.

"Exactly what? What do—"

"I agree with her," Millie says, pointing at me. "There is a void here as well that we need to fill first. We should absolutely not climb out. Not yet."

"What do you mean? Don't you want to get out of here?"

"What I mean is that we are together here, and maybe we should take another moment. With each other," Millie continues. She steps back, assessing the situation as if she's just seeing us for the first time. "There you are too, Emilia. The baggage I made you carry. There's just so much you both don't know."

"It's not like we've been stopping you from telling us," Em says. "Go crazy. I'm all ears."

"See, there. That. That's one thing. There's no reason for that."

"For what?"

"That attitude. That tough-girl facade. We carried it—you've been carrying it—for too long. A year has passed, dear. Let it go."

"Let it go? Are you fucking kidding me?"

I motion to Millie, so I can respond. I've got this.

"Whatever the truth is about Mom, you're still angry at Dad—I guess we all are—but he was just trying to protect you."

"Protect me? From what?"

"Probably from this." Millie points her knobby finger at each of us, eeny-meeny-miny-moe-style.

"From ourselves? That's totally stupid."

"No, not exactly from ourselves. From fighting with ourselves. From not letting ourselves find peace. As Emilia said before, I do believe that he thought that if he could convince us that we had nothing to do with the accident, it would be easier to move on."

I nod enthusiastically. I came to this realization in college, in a Russian literature class during my sophomore year, when I read a line in *Anna Karenina* that struck my innermost core with the profundity that things can only do when one is still young and everything in the world seems to be speaking to them.

In the novel, Stiva, Anna's brother, has been caught in an affair, and he moans something to the effect of "*she won't forgive me, and she can't forgive me. And the most awful thing about it is that it's all my fault—all my fault, though I'm not to blame. That's the point of the whole situation.*"

He was guilty as sin, that Stiva, but to me that wasn't the point. The point was that I felt the same about my dad. He was guilty, but he wasn't to *blame*. Well, technically, Stiva *was* to blame, but my dad wasn't. He was guilty of lying but that was not the most egregious part of the crime. That was on me, for me to carry alone. I decided right then that my dad had suffered enough.

Em isn't having it. "I don't believe that for a second," she says. "I don't care what you say, what parental bullshit you grant him as an excuse or whatever. The lie was for Dad, for his benefit, so he wouldn't have to feel guilty for the rest of his life that he let me drive his new car. If he was driving it and lost control, that's one thing. But if he let me drive a brand-new car just after it rained, that's another."

"Em," I say, reaching for her.

She slumps back into her corner, away from me. "Whatever."

"Don't *whatever* me," I say, and there is something in my tone that makes Millie sit up straight.

"Stop it," she snaps. "Both of you."

It is like when a teacher slaps a ruler on a desk or a lifeguard blows a whistle. Everything stills for a moment, even our breathing.

"Here's the bottom line," Millie says, when it is clear that she has our complete attention. "There is nobody but us here. And we are the same damn person. That's it. It is just me, me, and me. And as the eldest me, let me tell you something. It's not worth it."

She looks at me and Em. Our eyes are locked on her. She has our full attention, so she continues. "It's not worth waiting around our whole lives for someone to see us for who we are and continually punish them when they don't. That's what we do. Because whether or not Mom turned the wheel, regardless of how we remember it, we've always felt guilty, right? Ugly? Rotten? And maybe we are. But the bottom line is this: after seventy-seven years, I can tell you with full confidence that nobody else will ever see it like that. And they certainly wouldn't humor this idea that the great Sally Fletcher may have had some hand in it at all. Only we will know that. Maybe that is enough. We don't need the rest of the world to validate our story, but knowing there is someone else out there who believes me—even if that someone else is myself, twice over—makes me feel a little bit better. Do you not feel that?"

Em and I look at each other, and that's all that it takes.

Within seconds both of us, then all three, have tears running down our faces. Years and years of tears forcing themselves to be released.

Yes. We feel it too.

36

Good Times: Emilia

October 12
11:54 p.m.
Friendship Heights Metro
Washington, DC

The earth spins on its axis. It is almost midnight. The moon will soon begin its descent and the sun will start to rise. Etc. Etc. Inside the elevator, it is bright as day—brighter, in fact—and while sleep would be welcome, it isn't forthcoming.

The tears finally dried up and conversation between us has been flowing, but now it is starting to ebb. There is a welcome lightness between us, things are feeling less strained, but it takes endurance to wrestle one's demons. As things slow, Millie begins sawing at her nails with the offending nail file. May as well put it to some use, after all. The sound is soothing, to a point. At least it is something new to listen to, not a fluorescent buzz or the beat of our hearts.

Em has reverted to her position in the corner under the button panel, head forward as she pulls her hair in front of her face to search for split ends. I remember doing that. Lord, I spent hours like that quite literally splitting my hairs. I undo my messy bun and hold the hair band out to Em. "Here," I say. "It's just easier. You'll drive yourself nuts like that."

Em takes it and pulls her hair back into a ponytail. She feels me watching her. "What?"

"Nothing. It's just, you are very pretty. I know you don't think that, but you are. I mean, when I can see your face. When you aren't hidden behind all those bangs."

"It's true," Millie agrees. "So are you, Emilia. You are a very attractive woman. I never understood that. I could only see what was wrong with myself, not what was right. There is a lot that is right in the both of you."

Em thinks about this. It feels nice to hear a compliment she can actually accept. "Can I ask you something, Millie?"

"Of course."

"Why did you do that…what was it called, that frozen face thing?"

"Your face is not really all that bad, now that I'm getting used to it," I say, trying to soften Em's question. "And be nice, Em. It isn't easy getting old. You'll see."

Millie shakes her head. "Honestly, it wasn't a very good idea to have these injections. And you're correct, Emilia, but you literally don't know the half of it. It can be hard to see myself in the mirror sometimes. But that's not why I had these treatments. Maybe not consciously, but I suppose I thought that if I could see a little more of Mom in me, maybe something would come of it, even if only for myself."

I study Em's face—my face—for a moment and then look at the face of my future. "You know, that makes sense to me. Mom is the only other person who could attest to the truth. You needed to see her. We needed to see her."

"Okay," says Em, turning to Emilia. "So tell the truth then. What do you see when you see Mom in Millie?"

I take a few moments to consider Millie's face. The similarities with our mother are uncanny, which is kind of funny since of the three of us, I am the one closest to the age she was when she died, but I never saw my mother in myself. Maybe I haven't looked hard enough. Or maybe it is because Millie is now the one with the light-colored hair and coiffed style. Maybe it's her tailored, elegant attire. Maybe it is simply the fact that she exudes a little more confidence than the other two of us.

"I guess I see someone who wasn't perfect," I say. "No offense, Millie."

Millie isn't offended. "Nobody is," she says.

"Mom wasn't easy," I continue, looking at Millie as if I am

analyzing a painting. "I don't think I ever doubted that she loved me. I just doubted that she liked me."

"Do you think she would like you more now?" Em asks me. "I mean, as a grown-up?"

"Probably not," I say. "I have no career to speak of and my marriage is falling apart. I think she would like Sonya—she presents well—but I am guessing she'd probably be disappointed in how I turned out."

"Do you agree with that?" Em asks Millie.

Millie shrugs. "I imagine most parents secretly feel some disappointment in their grown children from time to time. You have all of these hopes and dreams for them. It is hard to take your ego out of it."

"Is that how you feel about Sonya?" Em asks.

"Yes," Millie starts to say just as I am saying no. We look at each other.

"Is that true?" I feel as if I've just been punched in the gut. "You are disappointed in Sonya?"

"It's more that I'm disappointed in myself. I didn't nurture our relationship as well as I should have. I was too distracted most of the time. I already told you, she's not very kind to me. I probably deserve it."

"But you can still be nicer to her," Em says. "It's not too late, is it?"

"I hope not."

"Will you give her the house?"

"I truly don't know," Millie says with a sigh. "Honestly, she might just take it and change the lock. But even if I did give it to her, I don't know if it would be enough to fix our relationship."

"It would be a start."

"Yes. That's probably true."

"Hang on," says Em. "Dad left you the house when he died. Did that change how you felt about him?"

I laugh. She's a sharp one, that Em. That's a good question, but I am not sure of the answer. "I just wish I hadn't let things get so toxic."

"Isn't that the truth," Millie agrees.

"So when do things start to feel better?" Em asks.

"Oh good Lord, Em. What is this, some kind of game of truth or dare?"

Millie laughs. "Now, that would be amusing. I dare you both."

"To do what?" Em asks.

"To play."

"You should go first, Em," Emilia says. "Given that you are already on a roll."

"Go first, as in you dare me, or I have to dare you?"

"Don't we need to spin a bottle to see who takes the turn?" Millie asks.

"Nah, I think Em should go. We can give her that. Em, ask us anything you want. Truth or dare. It can be either."

"Other than jumping out of that door, I can't think of any good dares, so hold on." Em thinks for a minute. "I could ask for a truth, I guess. But I don't think I want to know all that much more other than that everything is going to be okay, and Millie seems convinced that it will be. I don't know."

"Oh, come on!" I say. "It's the opportunity of a lifetime!"

"I know! But if I ask you about a good thing, it will take away the surprise, and if it's something bad, then I'll be living in dread."

"Fine," I say. "Then you have to make it a dare."

"I dare you to do what? You've already taken off half of your clothes."

"Touché," I say. "I'll dare Millie then. Millie, I dare you to sing to us, really loud."

"Ouch!" she says, because we all know full well what cacophony she will be imposing on us. "Fine, what song?"

"Sweet Caroline?" Em asks sheepishly. Embarrassing though it is, she knows we all love it. It was the last song that was played the night of Amy's bat mitzvah, and after that, she and Amy sang it all the time, until they didn't, of course. But still. We did love that song.

"I only remember the chorus," Millie says.

"So start with that."

"Okay. Here goes nothing." She takes a big breath and barks out the tune of Neil Diamond's "Sweet Caroline" and Em and I join in, creating a strange, off-kilter harmony that truly only we could love. "*Bum, bum, bum...*"

Soon the three of us are holding hands and dancing around. We are getting so exhausted, so punch-drunk that it builds and builds into a dervish of sorts and we all start laughing so hard we have to grab at the handrails to hold steady.

When things finally settle down the mood shifts into a contented silence. We sit together in the middle of the floor, with knees touching as if we are having an underwater tea party.

"Truth?" Millie says, although nobody has asked. "I am so happy to reconnect."

"Me too," I say.

We smile at each other. Millie with her elegant white bob. Em with those wide brown eyes we can see now that the eyeliner has all rubbed off and her bangs are pushed back.

"Truth?" Em looks from me to Millie and back. "I just realized something. I just..." She pauses. We wait as she pulls together her thoughts. "You guys aren't so bad."

Millie and I practically fall over laughing.

"Anyway," Em says once we've gathered ourselves, "whatever happens, if we ever get out of here, that has to add up to something, right?"

"You know, dear," says Millie with a little wink. "I always knew you were smart. If you ask me, I believe it might add up to everything."

"I think—" I start to say, but the conversation is rudely interrupted by that all-too-familiar buzzing of the fluorescent light. "Are you fucking kidding me?"

The light shuts off.

"Apparently not," says Em in the darkness.

"Well," says Millie. "At least now maybe we can get some rest."

37

JUST EM

It is unsettling to wake up in pitch-black darkness, and for a brief moment Em is unsure of where she is. She pats the ground around her and feels the gritty texture of the hard, cold floor. Then she remembers. She feels almost relieved, for a moment. At the very least it is centering to be able to place herself.

How long has she been out? She has absolutely no idea. She doesn't recall drifting off. It must have been when Millie and Emilia were talking about Sonya, chattering like two gossipy girls at a slumber party. They fell into a pool of reminiscences, drowning in memories of seminal moments from the early part of their daughter's life. It was a bit much for Em, hearing about her own daughter's first steps, her first words, the time she did a lip-sync performance of a song by some singer called Lady Gaga at her elementary school talent show. Was that third grade or fourth? Millie and Emilia had been bickering about that. Seriously, it would have put any teenager to sleep. It put Em to sleep, but now she is very much awake.

"Emilia? Millie? Are you guys up?" she whispers softly. Her tongue feels sticky in her mouth when she speaks. She is so thirsty. "Emilia? Millie?" she whispers again.

There is no answer. Nothing. Not even a breath.

There is nothing.

Nothing.

Nothing.

"Millie? Emilia!" Em yells.

She stops and listens, trying to make out any vibration, any hint of the presence of her older selves. All she can hear is the percussive rhythm of her own heartbeat reverberating inside her head.

She calls for them again and again and doesn't stop calling until her voice starts to go hoarse. All the while she is frantically crawling about the rectangular space, patting the gritty floors and hard metal walls, blindly reaching out and trying to touch something, anything, in this hideous dark.

A steady breeze wafts in through the propped-open doors. It feels cool on her tear-drenched face, almost refreshing. Should she attempt to climb out? she wonders briefly before deciding she doesn't quite dare.

She finds her backpack in the opposite corner, zipped and packed as if a maid had tidied up her belongings. Her sweatshirt is folded and smells as sweet as if it has been professionally laundered. She hugs it and starts to cry.

She is entirely alone and the panic is building up fast. She curls back into herself, knees to her chest, and pulls the sweat-shirt over her head. She lets it tent over her for protection, although she isn't sure from what.

Nothing happens. Not for what feels like a very long time.

The darkness remains impenetrable. Is this what it was like for her mom? As the car continued to sink, did all light dissolve? Was this kind of absence of everything the last thing her mother ever experienced? What was she thinking about?

It surprises Em to realize now that she's never asked herself this before. She's thought about how scared her mother must have been, sure. But Em's greatest fear has been that in her mother's last moments she would have been cursing, frustrated and angry with Em as she so often was. So Em didn't go there until now, sitting here curled up and alone in the dark.

No. That's not what it was. She thinks about Millie, how she and her daughter aren't close, but she knows that while Millie may not like Sonya very much, she does love her. Em knows that one day when she is in Millie's place, if Sonya comes to her asking for the house, she will give it to her.

It is funny to think of that house so many years from now,

about how it will change, what will be the same. She promises herself that when the house is hers, she won't do what Emilia did. She won't freeze it in time. She will change the furniture, she'll plant lots of trees, she'll paint the yellow room whatever color she likes. Maybe a nice pale blue. That would be a good switch.

She thinks about this and thinks maybe she should try to convince her father they should do that now. They should stop treating the house like a shrine. If she ever gets out of here. If she sees him again. This thought scares her, because what if she doesn't? What if she dies here, if this is the end?

But she knows it's not. It can't be. Because of Emilia and Millie. She knows for sure that one day she will meet them again. It's a comforting thought. She actually liked them, after all that. Lord knows she misses them.

Life is so weird, Em thinks. If I like myself as I will be then, as Emilia and Millie, can I like myself now? Maybe. There's hope yet.

Something shifts, inside and out.

Em notices that the air has become thinner. There is a very subtle scent of burning dust, as if a space heater has been turned on after many months in storage. Something is happening. She knows it, she's sure of it, and her heart starts to race.

Quickly she pulls herself up to stand, and using the hand-rails as a guide she makes her way toward the open door, moving sideways with her arm outstretched and reaching until her hand hits the panel of buttons. She feels for round outlines and punches each one she can find.

An alarm sounds. It is deafeningly loud. Then a crackling sound of static, followed by a voice over the intercom.

A voice.

It is very distant, like an echo through a tunnel. But someone is there. Someone is asking if she is all right. Telling her to remain calm. It will be only a few minutes more.

So she stands there frozen, both out of fear and out of hope.

There is a clank. A clunk. The turning of gears.

What happens now? What happens next?

Whether it is one minute or ten, she will never be sure—a sudden jerk knocks her off balance for a beat and she has to steady herself before she hears the rattle of the chains doing their work.

Slowly, the elevator descends and the light from the station seeps in. A chime sounds, and the doors open all the way, a parting of curtains revealing the most ordinary thing.

Three people are standing across the threshold, waiting for her to step out so they can step in. One man in a suit. Another in jeans. A woman pushing a stroller. Make that four people if you count the toddler fussing in her seat.

Em hesitates. She looks back into the elevator, that stainless steel box that briefly contained almost the entirety of her life. She picks up her bag and tentatively steps through to the other side, unsure of her footing, as the other people step aside to let her out. Em wants to say something, tell them not to go in there, but she knows she is wrong. Nothing will happen to them. Nothing out of the ordinary, anyway. They will go on with their days.

The doors close behind her and she hears the chains chug in reverse.

She follows the path of rust-colored hexagonal tiles to the turnstiles. She flashes her student Metro pass and pushes her way through. The platform is still one more level down. Em takes the escalator down to the platform. The cavernous ceiling overhead arches upward, with rows of curved cement beams resembling ribs inside the belly of a whale. And from the mouth of the tunnel in the distance, the train rushes in.

It is heading north.

38

JUST MILLIE

Millie is still awake. The minutes tick forward in the dark, and Emilia and Em seem to have had no trouble falling asleep at all. She misses those days, that ability to sleep deeply enough to wake up fully refreshed. It is so rare now. One more thing that slipped away when she wasn't paying attention.

If only she could get herself a little more comfortable, this wouldn't be so awful, Millie thinks. But there is a deep comfort in being surrounded by her younger selves. She wishes she could see them, but even feeling their presence is fine.

She is grateful that she could share with them what little she did, that she could give them a small glimpse of their futures and some advice about her past, but there is so much more she wants to tell them.

Em, she wants to say, letting Dad love you is more important than making him believe you.

Emilia, you should smile more. You are so pretty. Still. Know that. Own that. And Joel is really not so bad. You are as much to blame as he is for the tension, probably more. Ease up. I wish I had.

Both of you, nobody will ever fully understand you, that's true. But does anyone ever truly understand anyone in this world? I am not so sure. So consider us lucky to have this three-dimensional view.

I wish I could tell you that things will be okay with Sonya. That the close relationship you have with her now will last. It won't. But I regret that I didn't work harder to make it work better. I am sorry for that. Maybe things will be different with little Sally. I am hopeful they will.

As for our mother, I am not here to tell you that she wouldn't have been disappointed in us. But I regret letting a hypothetical sentiment be the driver of my life. I can see that clearly now, and I thank you both for that.

If we ever do get out of here, let's embrace the brand new day. I know Mom's catchphrase was corny, but I do wish I had done a better job of taking it to heart. You still can.

Millie thinks about this. She smiles and closes her eyes, waiting for the sleep she knows will eventually come.

39

Just Emilia

When I wake up, my eyelids feel glued shut and I have to practically pry them open. Not that I can see anything anyway. It's still darker than night. I push myself up to sit and then pad around to find my purse, hoping I might find a bottle of eyedrops I somehow hadn't noticed before. I don't.

The light flickers back.

"Shit." I duck down to shield my eyes. I blink a few times to adjust, to try to generate some moisture. I look around.

Em is sound asleep, curled up into a feral fetal position like a cat hiding under a deck.

Millie, on the other hand, is sitting serenely with her legs stretched out and her ankles crossed in front of her as if she's sunning on a park bench. She looks almost refreshed. Elegant, even, the way she's tied that lavender scarf around her neck.

She smiles at me, looking a little wistful.

"Why are you so happy?" I ask.

"Just finding some peace with myself."

I have to laugh. Because, well, I suppose I like her too.

"So now what?"

"So I've been trying to sort this through. If you play it out, even if only one of us escapes, the other two will still live, yes?"

"Yes. We already discussed that. Are you becoming senile too?"

"Nope. I am fully lucid." Millie taps her head. "And I have an idea. What if we tie some of the jackets and shirts together and lower one of us down the drop? If it's not too far, great. If we get to the end of the rope, so to speak, we pull her back up. Nothing lost. Nothing gained."

As ideas go, I've heard worse. "But who goes down?"

"That's not a question. It has to be Em," Millie says, gesturing toward the girl. "She's the heart of our future."

"That is very Hallmark of you."

Millie crosses her arms and says sternly, "Come on, Emilia. Work with me here."

"Fine. She's also much lighter than either of us, so that helps. But yes, I get what you mean. Em lives, and assuming she's learned a thing or two in this space, we'll all be better for it."

"Exactly. But don't overthink it or you'll get stuck."

"I know. So should we wake her up?"

Millie shakes her head. "Let her rest a little longer. Assuming this works, she will have plenty of time. No need to rush."

"I can hear you," Em mumbles. "I'm awake now, thank you very much."

"Well, that was easy then," I say. I pull myself up and give Em a hand. She weighs next to nothing. "Please remember to eat more when you get out of here."

"Whatever," says Em with a big yawn. "Ugh, my mouth tastes so gross. How long was I out?"

"No idea."

"So take a look then, on that device of yours."

I sigh and pull out the phone. "That's weird," I say, tapping the screen to double-check what I am seeing. "It says it's 11:17 a.m. October 12."

"What?" Em and Millie say at the same time.

"Apparently time is going backwards now." I hold up the screen so they can see for themselves. "Maybe if we wait another minute, the elevator will start to move, and then the doors will open."

"Yeah," sniffs Em. "And I'm the queen of Sheba."

We wait.

The clock doesn't move.

"Oh, to hell with it," Millie says, standing up in her stocking feet. She walks over to the partially open door and braces her hands against the sides. A strong breeze blows the ends of the scarf backward, causing it to billow and flutter. It's as if she is a geriatric superhero, able to hold heavy steel elevator doors ajar.

"What are you doing?" Em asks.

"Just making sure there isn't a better option."

"Is there?"

"No," Millie says, stepping back.

"So," says Em. "I guess you are going to have to lower me down there, like some kind of reverse Rapunzel."

"Are you okay with that?"

Em shrugs. "Do I have another choice?"

She doesn't.

We gather up what we can—my shearling jacket, my urine-soaked shirt. Millie holds her hand out to Em. "Off with it," she says, and Em peels off her pants.

In short order, Millie ties together a strange approximation of a rope. A pant leg knotted to the wrist of the jacket; the other wrist knotted to another shirt, knotted to Millie's stockings, and so forth.

I take off my jeans—more length of fabric to add to the cause, and I stand there in my underwear, watching Millie do her magic with those knobbed hands. All assembled, her contraption extends a little more than the width of the elevator, maybe ten feet, max.

"Take my phone," I say to Em. "You can try to shine it, the flashlight, from the end, to see if you can make out a landing."

"And hold it with what? I need both hands to hold on."

"Your teeth?"

"All that money spent on orthodontia…" Em says. "Fine, I'll give it a try."

Millie secures one end of the knotted length of clothing and bags to the handrail and then pokes her head through the opening.

"Do you see anything?" Em asks. She walks over to Millie, grabbing the rail with one hand and the bottom of Millie's undershirt with the other, so she can pull her back in case she falls.

Millie shakes her head. "Nothing."

Em peers over. "It's so dark!"

"The power must still be off below," I say, crouching down next to them.

"No, it's like it has a force," explains Millie, still staring straight out. As she says this, she sticks her head farther through the door, and then, just like that, her body is ripped forward as one might fall out of an airplane a thousand feet up, pulling all of our belongings down with her as she is sucked out of sight. It happens so fast she doesn't even have time to scream.

But Em screams.

She has let go of the shirt and it is too late. "Millie!" she cries, and not thinking rushes to the opening to look out to see where her older self has gone.

In doing so, she too is swept away. Here and then not.

The doors gently close, as if in slow motion.

I am the only one that remains.

I push myself even deeper into the corner, reaching up to grab the handrails. My heart is beating so fast I can hardly think.

Instead, I scream. My voice ricochets off the steel walls as if the elevator were an echo chamber, as if I am screaming at myself. I look around frantically, but there is no door that Millie or Em could be hiding behind, no box to pop out of. It is just me, Emilia, alone and present tense, screaming in a voice that has been ground down by four decades and change.

Millie's patent leather bag is still in her corner, the contents spilling out—a tube of lipstick, the wrapper from the Kleenex, yet another ballpoint pen. I sweep it up and put it all back into place, unsure of what else to do. The elevator floor is covered with detritus. Pens. Crumpled-up receipts. Piles of the clothing we have shed. Em's sweatshirt is in a heap under the button panel. I pick it up and hold it close to my face, wiping away the tears that are streaming down.

Without the others, without their body heat, the space is starting to cool. I pull on the sweatshirt, which is large even for me.

I inhale deeply, and then collapse onto the floor.

Time passes, as it does. I am stuck in here, all by myself, sealed for eternity inside a thick metal cage.

I am so hungry. I pat the space around me as if there might be something to find.

There, shoved in the crack where the wall meets the floor right next to me, is the pen we had shoved in the door. I reach over to get it. I turn it in my hand and notice the cut on my palm. A small scab is starting to form. I pick at it. I can almost hear myself chastising Sonya when she does the same.

Sonya.

There needs to be a course correction, I know that. I do like Millie, I really do, but I know I can't become her, not entirely. I need to become a Millie who has at the very least an amicable relationship with Sonya. I need to be a Millie that Sonya would want to have stay in the house.

But how does that happen? I am not fully sure, but I do know this: what happened to Millie and Sonya's relationship was never Sonya's fault. It was Millie's. It was mine. To change that, to start the flutter of the butterfly wings that will turn into a wave, I decide that if I ever get home, the first thing I will do is plant those trees before they die. I'll suggest to Joel that we let Sonya decide where to dig. It would be a compromised olive branch, but it is a start. Maybe after, we can go to the nursery together and pick out a few seedlings.

I hold the cut to my mouth. The faint metallic taste of the old blood seeps through.

Funny to think this is a scar I will have the rest of my life. At least now I will know where it is from.

Suddenly, there is a clang. A clunk. The turning of gears.

I sit up, snapping my head in each direction.

What is that?

The elevator shakes ever so slightly, but it may as well be an earthquake.

What happens now? What happens next?

It's simple, really. The light flickers and then floods back on, and in that illuminated space, more lit up than a surgical suite,

I see nothing. Just the bags I came in with, all packed up as if I'd just walked out of the store. But the sweatshirt, I still have it on, with the Washington Day School mascot emblazoned on the faded forest-green fabric.

Slowly I feel the elevator start its ascent. The lights above the button panel turn on. The red arrow is pointed up. And the neon letter changes from an M to an S. The street. There, the elevator comes to a halt.

I want to jump up but I am too exhausted to move. A chime sounds and the doors start to open. An even stronger light floods into the space, and for a moment I wonder if maybe, for all our talk of hell, this is heaven after all. But as the doors continue to slide apart and over the rigid metal threshold, I see the rust-colored hexagonal tiles. They are beautiful, I think, and will myself to stand. I grab my purse, leaving the other bags behind, and carefully step onto the landing.

A pulsing vibration comes from inside my bag, from my phone. I dig in to find it. Two missed calls. Two messages. *Emilia, where are you? Mom, are you there?*

I am here.

The clock says 11:18 a.m.

At the entrance to the Metro platform, a worker is holding a chain.

"Glad you got out, ma'am," he says. "Lots of mechanical troubles today." He shuts the gate behind me as I step out to the street.

I walk past a homeless man wrapped up in a plastic sheet, sleeping behind the rows of plastic newspaper kiosks. I stop and turn back. I pull the sweatshirt over my head and gently place it across his chest like a blanket. He opens his eyes, startled to find this middle-aged woman standing in front of him.

He struggles to sit up. "You okay there?" he asks.

"You know what?" I say. "I think I am. But thank you. It is kind of you to ask." And with that, I turn and walk down the street toward my house. Today is a brand new day.

ACKNOWLEDGMENTS

It took many years of fits and stops and dog walks to write this story, and I could not have completed it without the help of many wonderful people. First, this book is dedicated to my amazing and patient friend Tula Karras, who has heard more about *Just Emilia* than anyone else, always offering a sympathetic ear and a deft editorial eye. You are the best. Thank you to Jaynie Royal, Elizabeth Lowenstein, and the entire Regal House team for helping me take Emilia out of the elevator and into the world. Thank you to my Summer 2025 Frontlist cohort for the wonderful camaraderie. A special shout out to Miriam Gershow for all the wise words, and to the incomparable Laura Scalzo for introducing me to Regal House in the first place.

Many people generously read multiple drafts and gave me invaluable feedback, both about the book specifically and about the whole process of getting it into the world in general. I am deeply grateful for all the love and encouragement. Thank you to Hilary Black, Stephanie Cohen, Daniel Cohen, Andrew Cooper, Helen Dimos, Cara Dubroff, Alexis Gargagliano, Sasha Gottlieb, Jennifer Howze, Laura Lombardi, Richard Nash, Benjamin Oko, Daniel Oko, Erica Perl, Eric Roston, and Karen Yourish, and to Christina Willis Oko for the vigilant fine tuning.

Thank you to my 71 Raymond roomies, Barbara Magnoni, Lisa Colvin, and especially Jan Trasen for the eleventh-hour edit. I definitely won the housing lottery with you three! The SFD Tenley chat group is a font of inspiration. Thanks for the daily fifteen minutes of fun. A super special thank you to Mary Kay Zuravleff, Sophia Coudenhove, and Kimberly Stephens for all your input and wisdom and for sharing your writing with me. Thank you to my parents Sue and Arnold Cohen for the decades upon decades of support, and for letting me take over the back deck every summer. Miriam Weintraub, my partner in production and filmmaking crime, you always make me a better writer, whatever the format. Big thanks to Judge the Dog for keeping me company and to Cocoa the Cat for keeping my keyboard warm.

Laila and Jasper, you are my inspiration for everything good. I love you both to the moon and back infinite times over.

Michael, I am beyond lucky that I got lost (and found) with you in Paris all those years ago. I couldn't ask for a better partner to navigate this world with. I would, quite literally, be lost without you.

This project is supported in part by the DC Commission on the Arts and Humanities, which receives support from the National Endowment for the Arts.